INSPECTOR OTHMAN

Philip Garrard

ISBN: 099555871X
ISBN 13: 9780995558717

CHAPTER ONE

Chief Inspector Othman read the letter again:

Hi Othman

Remember me? I promised we would meet for coffee so I thought I'd drop you a line. It's been about a year since I left Cairo. Got myself a job in the British Museum as Junior Consultant Archaeologist. My home address is 39 Glebe Way, Barnes, London and my mobile hasn't changed.

It would be good to see you again if you thought about coming over here.

You must've heard the news about the assassination of the Head of MI5 – terrible business. They thought I had something to do with it but I'm now off the hook. Don't think they'll ever get to the bottom of it.

Looks like there's no stopping the Iraq war. Hope you're safe. Would be good to see you again if possible. Got this terrible malaise since Rob died. Could do with some cheering up if you get the time – and inclination.

Miss you
Rania Hakim
May 2004

Othman got up from his armchair and stared out the window. He gazed upon the famous Pyramids set against the backdrop of the desert and reflected on his situation. He often thought about Rania and her support in the Dr Rob Williams case. She really loved Rob but their relationship was shockingly terminated by his assassination prompted by his stand against the Iraq war. This wasn't the official line, of course, but Othman was sure this was the case. It didn't matter now. Rob's assassin had been killed, Rania had found herself a job in England and Othman had been promoted. At the same time John Wilkinson, Head of MI5, had been murdered by an Islamic extremist, or, at least, that was how it was presented in the press, and things had subsequently settled down – apart, of course, from the war which continued to rage in the Middle East.

Othman needed a break. He had many contacts in England having established them at university, and maybe a holiday was due. His family were mainly based in Khartoum and he'd no firm ties in Cairo. Perhaps it was time for a clean break. A holiday may kick start a new beginning. He could meet up with Rania and, who knows, something may spark up a friendship. In any case, it would be good to see her again and reacquaint himself with good old London town.

He phoned her and to his surprise she answered:

'Great to hear from you Othman, how are you?'

'Fine' he said 'how are you?'

'It's all working out well, when are you coming over?'

'As it happens I'm owed quite a bit of leave and do you know something? - I'm going to take it. I need to finish a few jobs here and will give you a call when I'm on my way.'

'Great' Rania said 'look forward to seeing you.'

'Me too.'

Othman finished work early that day and made his way across Cairo to see his Sudanese friends who ran a launderette business. He'd stayed at a hotel in Giza for the last few days while on a mission to catch some thieves who'd stolen pieces of rock from the Pyramids. This was illegal but didn't stop well organised gangs from taking and selling bits of rubble for profit. The problem had got worse, especially as tourists were being forced into buying the stuff, so the authorities brought in Othman to sort it out. This he'd done successfully and needed a new purpose.

He arrived at the launderette and was greeted by a tall, distinguished black man in his fifties. His curly hair was completely white and matched his teeth which gleamed in a magnificent smile:

'Hi Othman'.

'Hi Mo, how are you?'

'Great, come in, come in. Magda and the kids are waiting for you. We've got chicken in the oven and freshly squeezed orange juice in the fridge.' He motioned Othman to the back of the launderette where the living quarters consisted of a large kitchen/diner, three bedrooms and a bathroom upstairs.

'Sounds great.'

Mohammed Ishmail was an old family friend who'd served in the Sudanese forces in the government's fight against gangs of ruthless rebels in the Khartoum suburbs. He was about six feet seven inches tall, lean, muscular, close shaven with a scar running down the right side of his face. 'What's happening my friend?' asked Mo.

'Oh, the usual, catching the bad guys and getting paid for it.'

'Right, come in here and sit yourself down. Magda will be down soon.' He paused... 'Look, before she does, there's bit of a problem.' His face took on a more stern expression.

'I'm listening.'

'She's got the big C, breast cancer in the early stages. Problem is we can't afford the treatment and Magda is just putting her head in the sand.'

'I'm sorry Mo, when did you find out?'

'About two weeks ago, when we got the test results. We've been trying to book her in for an operation but the waiting list is too long. I'm worried she's going to miss out so I...'

'Hi Othman'. Magda burst into the room as if she'd been listening and didn't want to hear any more of what was being said.

'Hi Magda, how are you?'

'I'm fine. Don't worry about what Mo's telling you.'

'But you have to get treatment darling, we have to find a way.'

'Nonsense, don't be burdening Othman with our worries. He's got other things to think about.'

'Look Magda, you're my closest friends and you've helped me out on a number of occasions. Let me help you now. I've got no responsibilities. How much will this operation cost?'

'We couldn't ask you to give us money Othman. We 're not your family and you owe us nothing' said Magda.

'You are my family, you need this operation and if you can't afford it, I want to help.'

Before anybody could say anything else Mo's children ran into the room. In fact, they weren't children but teenagers. Rashid was 16 and Chinaz was 14. They were beautiful young adults projecting a vitality which immediately lit up the room. Rashid was intelligent, calm and serene while Chinaz was wild, vivacious and outgoing despite entering her pubescent years. They always became excited when Othman came round as he told them stories of capers in which he'd had involvement. To make them interesting he always exaggerated the plot to hold their attention - making the story line credible to ensure a particular principle or moral were highlighted as he built up to a dramatic crescendo. The two of them gasped in disbelief as he developed the theme and clapped uncontrollably as he reached his finale – and some kind of moralistic conclusion. One such story involved his childhood and he decided to relate this now to break the awkward silence which followed upon their entering the room.

'Right, sit down you two and I'll tell you a true story' said Othman.

'Go on then' said Rashid 'but make it believable. The last one you told us turned out to be utter nonsense'.

'That's a bit harsh' said Othman 'You were impressed at the time, weren't you?'

'Not really, we were just being polite' Chinaz said with a twinkle in her eye.

'Okay, here goes. I was brought up in a village on the outskirts of Khartoum as you probably know. The countryside was breathtaking with escarpments, ravines and rivers running through valleys like meandering snakes finding their way to the many lakes and seas of the Sudan.' The two of them looked at each other and giggled. 'What's the matter?' asked Othman. 'There are no seas in the Sudan uncle, you're already making it up.' 'Don't be so ridiculous' said Othman 'let me continue... my father owned a small farm where he kept goats, cows and chickens. He loved these animals even though he had to slaughter half of them to feed his family. The other half he sold in the local market. However, he developed a unique relationship with one of his chickens. In fact, he kept it as a pet and the two became so attached that he didn't have the heart to throttle the poor thing at the annual Eid festivities. Instead he kept it alive on a year by year basis. Even more strange than this – he trained the bird to sit on his shoulder rather like the parrot perching on Long John Silver, as described by Robert Louis Stephenson in his novel 'Treasure Island'. My father would walk around the village attending to his chores and talking to his neighbours oblivious of the chicken perched on his shoulder. The bird became part of him. It became an extension of his personality. At night he would return it to the pen only to be greeted first thing in the morning with a fluttering of wings and a furious clucking resulting in the birds return on my father's shoulder. Time passed and my father grew old; but so did the chicken, inspired, I think, by my father's love which prolonged its life beyond that which was normal for a fat feathered bird. The two were inseparable even when my father was close to death. The extraordinary thing is this; when my father was lying in his open coffin, all his friends and relatives lined up to show their respect. And guess who was at the end of the queue?... Yes, you've got it right - my father's chicken - who, when it came to his turn, miraculously flew on to the edge of the coffin, clucked several times and died falling into the coffin next to my father. People thought it was a miracle and we all decided that the bird must be buried with my father. And so he was and to this day, if you visit my father's grave and listen very carefully, you will hear the sound of clucking coming from the earth.'

'And what's the moral of this story uncle Othman?' asked Chinaz.

'The moral is - never believe what your uncle tells you.' jeered Mo.

'That's not fair Mo, at least half that story is true.'

'What half?' Rashid asked.

'The bit where I talk about my father's death...he did die, he was placed in an open coffin and we did eat chicken at the celebrations!'

'So the chicken wasn't buried with your father?' asked Rashid.

'No but you can still hear the clucking noises if you stand near his grave.'

There was a short silence as everybody looked at each other in disbelief. Then everybody laughed including Othman who'd achieved another success in his nonsense story telling albeit this time at his late father's expense!

They all sat round the table in good spirit eating chicken and rice discussing days gone by and how things had changed over the last 25 years or so. When they finished the siblings went to their rooms and the atmosphere changed. Othman offered, once again, to pay for Magda's cancer treatment to which she declined saying she was happy to wait her turn.

'Look, the offer's there, if you change your mind. The quicker you address the problem the better because it's easier to treat this thing earlier than later.'

'We know Othman and we thank you. We'll think about your kind offer and let you know' said Mo.

'Another thing, I'm planning to take a holiday in the UK. Got some friends I want to catch up on and fancy taking a break from everything.'

'We don't blame you' said Magda 'when do you plan going?'

'As soon as possible, but don't want to go until we get you sorted Magda. Go to the private clinic straightaway and tell me how much it's going to cost. Tell them I'm your benefactor and give them my mobile number.'

'But Othman, you don't have...'

'Nonsense' Othman interrupted 'you are my family and I owe you for helping me out in the Dr Rob Williams case.'

'But we got paid for that' Mo said.

'Not enough' replied Othman as he got up and approached the front door.

They all hugged each other and Othman took his leave making a clucking noise, to everyone's delight, as he made a dramatic chicken-like exit.

CHAPTER TWO

Nigel Francis sat in his car watching the rain splatter on his windscreen anticipating the next rise and fall of intermittent wiper blades which would enable better focus on the traffic ahead. He stopped at a zebra crossing and let the commuters hurry across as they made their way to their offices - heads down, some holding newspapers to shield their heads, others holding umbrellas - all oblivious to his observing them closely as if he were on surveillance duty.

Nigel had met Othman at university and they had become good friends. They played football for the first eleven during winter and were opening batsmen during summer. The Sudanese have never been renowned for their cricket prowess but Othman was the exception to the rule – he excelled in anything to do with ball coordination and proved to be a competent all-rounder. Nigel on the other hand, whilst not so gifted, was driven by the desire to win and, although clumsy at times, threw himself into battle no matter what the sport. They made a good team. Othman was quick and skilful in front of goal while Nigel was the grafting provider in midfield. In cricket, Nigel was the 'teeth clenched' number one batsman, determined to stay at the crease in Geoffrey Boycott style, while Othman was the elegant stroke maker, reminding spectators of the great David Gower.

They did most things together, having similar senses of humour, and became a formidable duo when it came to partying and girls - although Nigel was the more dominant partner in matters of alcohol abuse and general revelling. When they left university they both joined respective police forces and progressed up the ranks to Inspector status. That has been the situation ever since. Nigel married a young marketing executive but the two divorced following a dispute over the interpretation of a 'work/life balance'! Othman remained single.

Nigel gazed at the pedestrians as they passed his car. Some of them looked his way, others looked to see where they were heading – all of them were in a hurry and anxious to get out of the rain. He noticed one particular lady in her thirties. She was wearing a stylish raincoat and held a small umbrella over her head. She had beautiful long black hair and a complexion indicating Middle Eastern origins. Nigel recognised her but couldn't remember where he'd seen her before. In the papers perhaps, or in a magazine. She was quite distinctive – tall, upright with an intriguing face which, although not beautiful, was stunning in other ways. As she passed, she briefly stopped and glimpsed at him in his car. She then hurried away and carried on with her journey. The zebra crossing cleared and he decided to follow her. He had a spare half hour having finished an early morning assignment involving an incident at Holborn Station, and wanted to satisfy his curiosity. The traffic was very dense, it being 8.45 in the morning with rain pelting down making surfaces slippery, so he was able to keep track of this mysterious woman until she reached the British Museum. She turned into the gates and continued walking towards the main entrance. Nigel parked his unmarked police car on double yellow lines and waited at the steps leading up to the Museum. After about one minute, the lady came out of the main doors holding what looked like a bunch of keys. She then walked along the front of the building until she vanished into a side entrance. That's it! She works at the Museum. Her name is Rania something and she was suspected of assassinating the Head of MI5 one year ago. All charges were dropped for lack of evidence. It was in all the newspapers. That's where he'd seen her before.

Nigel returned to his car soaked to the skin and made his way back to the station on Theobalds Road. On arriving he checked himself in and made his way to the canteen for a cup of coffee. He sat down with two other plain clothed police officers. He knew these two very well having worked with them for the last three years.

'Morning John, morning Lyn, how's it going?' he asked as he sat down at the small formica-covered table which needed replacing.

'We're fine Nigel' responded Lyn. 'What have you got for us today?'

'Nothing interesting, I'm afraid. I want you Lyn to speak to that guy in Hatton Garden and get a better description of the main witness – any details of where we can find him would be useful. John, I want you to speak to the staff at Holborn Station and find out what they know. I've got a feeling the robbery at

Hatton Garden is somehow connected to someone working at that station.'

'What do you mean?' asked John.

'Well, the guy down at Hatton Garden reckons one of the thieves was wearing a standard underground shirt and tie, although how he noticed that in the middle of a raid is beyond me. Still, we have to follow it up.'

'And what will you be doing handsome?' asked Lyn. Lyn was about 45 and, apart from being a pretty good investigator, was the station's cougar. She was buxom with short black hair, made up eyes, painted lips and a look which said 'have a go if you think you're hard enough'!

'I'm going to do a bit of scouting around in the basement. Do you remember that guy from MI5 who was shot? Well, one of the suspects was called Rania from Baghdad. Do you remember?'

'Yeah' said John 'she was in all the newspapers. Case was dropped though.'

'Right. Well I saw her this morning. She passed in front of me on a zebra crossing and then went to the British Museum.'

'So what' John said 'the case is closed.'

'I know. Call it curiosity. I just want to track down the newspapers in the basement to remind me of the case.'

'Why?' Lyn asked.

'Just curiosity Lyn... and a hunch I've got.'

'You know what they say about curiosity Nigel?'

'What's that?'

'It killed the cat.'

'I know. I'm not going to spend too much time on it as I've got to prepare a report for the chief for this afternoon's meeting. Any way you two, we've got a police service to provide so go out there and serve'!

John and Lyn got up from their chairs and made for the exit. As Lyn walked past her fellow officers she swung her buttocks in dramatic style so as to provoke friendly sniggers from both sexes:

'You're in the wrong job Lyn. You should've been a 'tom.'

'Get stuffed' she retorted 'otherwise I'll claim sexual abuse!'

'You'll lose your case as we're the victims having been deeply traumatised by the swinging of your arse!'

Lyn made her final exit by giving her admirers the one finger sign.

Meanwhile, Nigel took his leave and made his way to the basement where all records, including newspapers and journals, were kept. It was a dingy room with files stacked in metal shelves which had been constructed in the sixties and painted green to match, it seems, the decaying plaster falling off the walls. Nigel looked for the newspaper section and found it at the end of the room where the light was dim. He tracked down 2003 editions and narrowed his search to April and May. He had a feeling Sir Michael Wilkinson had been shot around that time.

After about an hour he found an article in the Times (30th May 2003) which read:

HEAD OF MI5 KILLED

Sir Michael Wilkinson, Head of MI5, was shot several times in the chest yesterday morning at around 9.00 a.m. The assassin was in Islamic dress and wore a burkha making identification impossible at this stage. The chauffeur describes the incident as a callous act of murder. He states that while he was waiting for Sir Michael in the basement car park a figure dressed in black appeared as Sir Michael tried to get into his car. He (Sir Michael) looked up and was shot several times in the chest. The assassin was thought to be female. The chauffeur was then ordered by the figure to drive her to Waterloo station at which point she left the car. He then phoned the police. Investigations continue.

Nigel then found another article dated 10th June 2003:

IRAQI ARCHEOLOGIST SUSPECTED OF MI5 KILLING

In a possible act of revenge a Ms Rania Hakim from Iraq is suspected of killing Sir Michael Wilkinson on 29ᵗʰ May 2003. It is reported that she denies the allegations saying that the evidence is circumstantial and no more than conjecture.

Reliable sources have reported that Rania Hakim was a close friend of the scientist, Dr Rob Williams who was killed in suspicious circumstances in Cairo on 10th March 2003. Ms Hakim thought MI5 were responsible although no supporting evidence was found to justify such a connection. It is believed that she secured a job at the British Museum and on 29ᵗʰ May 2003 murdered Sir Michael. Further evidence to support her connection is in the form of a photograph of Sir Michael which, as witnessed by the chauffeur, was pinned on to his jacket by the assassin. This photograph was originally owned by a former MI5 operative, Miss Katerine O'Reilly and was thought to be a gift from Sir Michael. Miss O'Reilly was killed by the same anonymous agent who murdered Dr Rob Williams. Accordingly, there is a connection between Ms Hakim and MI5 although whether this is sufficient evidence to 'point the finger' has yet to be established.

The only witness, Sir Michael's chauffeur, could not identify Ms Hakim as being the assassin and the latter has put forward alibis to corroborate her movements on that day. Investigations continue.

Finally, Nigel read the article dated 30th June 2003:

ARCHEOLOGIST CLEARED OF MI5 MURDER

The Crown Prosecution Service has confirmed that there is insufficient evidence to call for trial the named suspect, Ms Rania Hakim, for the murder of Sir Michael Wilkinson. In a statement issued to day the Service is satisfied that as no positive identification could be made by the chief witness, and in the light of corroborative evidence provided by two alibis, Ms Hakim could be eliminated from enquiries. The case against her is therefore dropped. Investigations continue.

In an interview with Ms Hakim she states: 'I am so grateful for the fair judicial system operating in the UK and I'm overcome with joy that the truth of my innocence has been established. I now look forward to the future in my new home and hope that I can make a worthwhile contribution to the cultural well-being of this wonderful country.'

Nigel pondered over the papers and then took copies of the relevant articles. He wasn't convinced of Ms Hakim's innocence and, more to the point, didn't believe the authorities had done enough before submitting the case to the CPS. How did she get that photograph, If in fact she was the murderer, and from whom? He smelt a rat.

CHAPTER THREE

Rania's phone rang just as she was sitting down to have her first cup of coffee of the day. It was Othman who told her he was on his way over and had booked himself a room in a hotel near Russell Square. They agreed to meet each other the next day at 12 by the entrance of the British Museum.

Rania was just about to get up when her boss, Professor Lear, touched her shoulder to indicate that he wanted to speak to her. He sat down and gazed at her.

The professor was Lear by name and leer by nature! He was about 55, had long flowing grey hair and sported a neatly clipped moustache which he'd dyed black. He resembled the pirate Captain Morgan and believed he had been Errol Flynn in a previous life. He fancied himself a 'lady's man' and took every opportunity to woo members of the opposite sex like some Shakespearian character in the hope that one of them would swoon into his arms and beg him to make love to her. Unfortunately his flattery had got him no where apart from a grievance from a girl in accounts who'd found his antics offensive. This resulted in an embarrassing session with the HR Director who told him to temper his advances. Such a warning had no effect at all and he continued to flatter, touch and generally 'creep' round any female who took his attention. Rania was no exception and today the professor was in a rampant mood.

'Hello my dear, you're looking exquisite today. I just needed a few seconds to gaze into those sensuous eyes. Please forgive me for I am but a slave to your beauty and wit and cannot wait a minute longer to tell you my good news.'

'And what's that?' Rania asked, who never took her boss seriously, 'you're leaving the Museum?'

'How cruel you are my pretty, do you not treasure every moment of my being with you?'

'No professor, I don't... now get on with your good news, I've got work to do.'

'Unforgiving girl, after all my compliments and flattery you still choose to thwart my advances with cutting remarks. My good news is this - tomorrow you and I will be in charge of the Greek Exhibition on the ground floor. We can work together hand in hand. What do you think of that my Iraqi wild flower?'

'Great, but I've got an appointment at 12, so I hope you can take a later break.'

'Of course I can, but it worries me you have an appointment – with whom may I ask?'

'You may ask kind sir but I'm not obliged to tell you. What I do and with whom I do it during my lunch break is of no concern of yours unless, of course, I bring the reputation of the Museum into disrepute. Only time will tell whether my activities tomorrow will jeopardise the image of this great establishment.'

'You tease me to utter despair. I take it you will be meeting a man which means my chances of fulfilling your desires are diminished as, knowing my bad luck, this man will be young and handsome and, dare I say it, more preferable to me.'

'You may say whatever you like but what I do and who I meet during lunch breaks is for me to know and for you not to know. I bid you adieu great boss.' With that Rania took her leave and hurried towards the ladies as her bladder was about to burst.

In the afternoon she decided to take a look at the exhibition and took the lift down to the ground floor. The floor was crowded with people. As she passed the cafes she noticed some very tempting cakes displayed on an elaborate stand and pondered whether she should or shouldn't. She'd been on a keep fit regime for the last couple of months and had lost a couple of pounds - she didn't want to reverse all the good work she'd undertaken on the treadmill. Just one cake wouldn't make any difference, she thought, and made a step towards the cake stand. As she was about to speak to the assistant a familiar voice bellowed across the dining area:

'You're not going to ruin that lovely figure are you my little Arabian wild flower?' The professor came running to her.

Oh no, it's him again, the predatory professor, performing at his best in front of everyone. 'Er no, of course not silly, I was just about to enquire about the origins of this beautiful cake stand. I think it's Victorian, don't you?'

'Let me see' said the professor, lapping up all the attention from the customers who must have thought he was the mad scientist from Spielberg's 'Back to the Future' movie. 'No, it's not Victorian Rania. In actual fact, it's Art Deco. You can tell by the way these carved ladies are practically naked, with only shreds of clothing covering their naughty bits.' He smiled at the onlookers who'd assembled around him and waited on his every word (at least that's what he thought they were doing).

Everything has to come down to sex when dealing with Professor Lear. You'd think by now he'd got the school boy talk out of his system. 'Oh really professor, I would never have guessed' Rania said 'anyway what are you doing down here. I thought you had more important things to do.' The onlookers began to disperse.

'What could be more important than talking to you. Besides, as we're partners, I thought I would join you in surveying the exhibition. That's why you're down here isn't it?'

'Yes' said Rania with a hint of resignation in her voice. 'Shall we go in then?'

'Here hold my hand. Don't want you getting lost' the professor said.

'Thanks but no thanks professor. If you don't behave, I'm calling the police.'

'All right all right, only joking. Let's take a look at these naked torsos. You lead, I'll follow.'

The exhibition was superbly lighted with the stone figures illuminated against the very dark background. In fact, there were no ceiling lights at all, only foot lights placed strategically on the ground to highlight the ancient statues in great detail revealing every fold in the clothing and every muscle in the torso. It was quite eerie in one sense as the hall would've been in complete darkness had it not been for the illuminated figures looming up from the ground casting mysterious shadows in some areas while lighting up the hall in others. There were dark corners which looked like black holes; dark areas not occupied; dark spaces not filled – it was best to follow the crowd rather than enter these 'nooks and crannies'. Who knew what or who would be there? May be a monster or a security guard or maybe even a professor? As Rania pondered these questions, out jumped the man himself from the shadows hoping to give her a fright or at least impress her with his dubious sense of humour.

'Don't do that you silly man. Act like a professor for once. It's like taking out a child.'

'You know you love my impish ways, don't deny it.'

'I don't and I do. Now just leave me alone before I claim harassment. I need to take notes on the background of each statue and so do you, so you better get on with it.'

'No need my dear. Follow me; listen and learn.'

The professor switched to serious intellectual mode and went round each figure giving a comprehensive analysis of the origins and, indeed, purpose of each sculpture. He knew all the relevant dates, the types of stone, the sculptor, the circumstances surrounding the creation and the reason for its creation in the first place. He had switched from clown to intellect within a split second. Rania was impressed and took copious notes. Pity he was a buffoon most of the time!

He finished his lecture with a Shakespearian bow and made his exit leaving Rania in the dark with just an illuminated exit sign in her vision. She made her way to this exit, opened the door and was immediately greeted by a good looking man in a suit.

'Rania Hakim?' he asked.

'Who wants to know?' she replied.

'I'm Nigel Francis from the Metropolitan Police. I'm sorry to disturb you at work but may we have a chat?'

CHAPTER FOUR

Mohammed and Magda sat in the waiting room which was located at the front of the private clinic. They'd managed to make an appointment the day after Othman left them. The room was appropriately decorated with ceramic floor tiles and the occasional Turkish rug positioned under small coffee tables which supported magazines like Vogue and Lancet. The walls were covered with pictures showing romantic Middle Eastern scenes with setting suns, palm trees and sandy dunes serving as backgrounds to various birds of prey. The staff were all dressed in white with the nurses wearing a stylish hat displaying some sort of medical emblem which, supposedly, differentiated them from the administrative staff.

Magda was nervous. She pretended reading a magazine; looked around the waiting room; shuffled her feet and smiled at every member of staff as they passed her. She could feel her hands sweating. Her mouth was dry although she didn't want to make the short trip to the water dispenser for fear of losing her place. She looked at Mohammed in desperation – willing him to make it better. But he couldn't. He just smiled and held her hand tightly. 'Not long now' he said. 'Soon it will be over and we can go home'.

Magda looked at the patients as they left the consultant rooms. Some were smiling having received good news. Others looked agitated whilst others had blank expressions resulting, she suspected, from hearing bad news. She had already received the bad news. All she wanted was some reassurance, some 'light at the end of the tunnel', some kind voice saying that everything would be all right and she had nothing to worry about. It was the waiting that got to her; the pondering over the 'what ifs'; the preparation for hearing the worst. Unfortunately, Magda was a 'glass half empty' person – always expecting the worst so that when it came it wouldn't be a surprise. She clutched hold of Mohammed's hand and quietly prayed to God.

'Mrs Ishmail?' a nurse asked. 'Come this way my dear. Do you want to come as well sir? That's fine. Both of you follow me.'

This is it, Magda thought to herself. No going back now. It's now or never. She wanted to be a million miles away as she followed the nurse down the corridor. The journey went on forever. She wanted to tell someone she was petrified, that she had had enough, that she wanted to go home, that she didn't want to hear bad news, that the cancer would go away... 'Come in Mrs Ishmail, take a seat' said the consultant as the nurse ushered them into his room. 'And you Mr Ishmail, sit with your wife.'

Mr Gustav was a German breast cancer specialist who'd spent the last 30 years practising in Cairo. He was an eminent physician in his field having undertaken advanced research in both England and the USA. He was about 55, tall and handsome – a silver fox with grey hair swept back from his forehead and resting on his collar.

'I have read your reports Mrs Ishmail and have to tell you that you have an aggressive cancer as well as an unusual one. I think it is in the middle stages and the good news is that it can be treated.'

'Will I be cured completely?' asked Mrs Ishmail.

'I don't know at this stage Mrs Ishmail but I do know that you need to have chemotherapy as a matter of urgency.'

'I thought it was in the early stages?'

'Yes, I can understand how the results could be interpreted in that way, but I believe it is more advanced which means that we must act quickly.'

Magda began sobbing. She could only see the dark side.

'Now, now Mrs Ishmail. You must have hope and be positive. Your cancer can be treated. It's not as if it's untreatable. If all goes well your tumour will be reduced to such an extent that an operation will be possible. After that you will probably need a course of radiotherapy. I know this is difficult but have faith in modern technology. I have seen many women like you make a full recovery.

'When can treatment start?' asked Mohammed.

'Well, that's a bit of a problem Mr Ishmail. You see your wife's tumour is quite unusual and although she could be treated in Cairo, she would have better chances in Germany or France or in the UK.'

'Why's that?'

'Because they have more up to date technology to deal with this kind of cancer. As I've said your wife's tumour is rare and will respond more effectively to the specialised equipment in Europe. Unfortunately, Egypt cannot afford this equipment and can only give your wife the standard treatment.'

'Say if she just had the standard treatment. What would this mean?'

'Her chances of success would be reduced by anything up to 25%. Look, I know a specialist in London who could oversee your wife's treatment using the latest technology. I will give you his details. If you're interested I will let him know and forward your records. If you're not interested, then let me know and we'll start chemotherapy straight away. Either way, I'm afraid it will be costly. Mrs Ishmail, your best chance of recovery is to use the latest technology. Unfortunately, we don't have the best equipment here so my advice is to go to London. I'm sorry If I'm sounding blunt, but I have to give you the best advice I can so that you have the best chance of a cure. If you do nothing, of course, the cancer will get worse and you will die. So you have to decide quickly what you want to do.'

'But what does this specialised treatment actually do?'

'On the chemotherapy side, the new drugs are far more focussed and penetrative. They are more expensive of course but can do the job more effectively without too many side effects – although, having said this there would be some. The same goes for the radiotherapy. The beams are more focussed and only affect the cancerous cells, leaving the non-cancerous cells unaffected. With regard to the operation, robotic keyhole surgery can be used which is more precise and allows the patient to recover very quickly. Now, I'm not saying that you would benefit from all these new developments – because that will depend on the specialist's recommendations and plan of action. What I can say is this – if you receive treatment in Cairo, you will not benefit from any of these new technologies. You will feel sick after chemotherapy sessions and you will lose your hair. You will not benefit from the latest advances in either keyhole or robotic surgery. It's the same for radiotherapy – you will not receive such an accurate treatment. It would be more of a scatter gun approach with non- cancerous cells being killed off making you feel tired and uncomfortable.

'Thank you Mr Gustav. You have been honest with us. We must talk to Othman our friend and benefactor to see whether he can help us with the costs. Could you give us some indication of what these will be?'

'I will give you the rough costs of both Cairo and London treatments. The Cairo treatment will be based on standard costs. The London treatment will be based on latest technology costs. Of course, if you go to London you must think about the cost of flights, travel and accommodation and factor these into your budget.'

'Yes, of course.'

'If you go back to the waiting room, I'll prepare some statements for you. I'll only be about half an hour. You can then speak to your friend and let me know what you want to do tomorrow. Time is of the essence, so please don't delay.'

Magda and Mohammed went back to the waiting room and waited. They were both silent, stunned by the news and worried by what the future may have in store for them.

━━◁+ +▷━━

When they arrived home, they stared at the statements which had been provided by Mr. Gustav. The total cost for the standard treatment was estimated to be £150,000. The specialised treatment in London would amount to £285,000. Both statements included a set of assumptions surrounding the number of chemotherapy and radiotherapy sessions, the operation itself and the aftercare. These were staggering amounts and made both Mohammed and Magda wince. This added to Magda's depression; she got up from her chair and listlessly stared at the pigeons who were frolicking about in the bushes in the backyard. They didn't have a care in the world apart from flying around looking for food. At that moment Magda wished she were a bird because all she wanted to do was to fly away.

'Let's phone Othman and see what he thinks' said Mohammed.

━━◁+ +▷━━

Mr Gustav phoned his counterpart in London. James Nathan had been a young aspiring specialist who had gained expertise in the latest developments in cancer treatment. He was in his thirties, arrogant and bearded; fiercely ambitious and a bad loser. He'd recently been rejected for promotion by a major London hospital and had lost out to an old rival, albeit the latter was twice his age. Disillusioned with the NHS he had aspirations to run his own clinic where he wouldn't have to pander to the unwritten code of the 'old boy network.' He used this network to suit his needs but secretly despised the 'old boys' for their incompetence and smugness. His bitterness had made him more arrogant and determined – determined to be a success both financially and professionally no matter what the cost and by any means.

Educated at Eton and Cambridge, James Nathan benefitted from a privileged background having parents who were successful in business with connections in Royalty and, indeed, the House of Lords. The family had made major contributions to the Conservative Party and had financed many marketing projects. James wanted more. He was not prepared to rest on his family's laurels preferring to make a name for himself on his own account. At university he'd excelled as a sportsman and tended to make friends on the basis of their usefulness to his personal ambitions. One such friend was a Thomas

DeVelt who went on to become an MI5 operative. The two had kept in touch. They had a lot in common – ambition, ruthlessness...and greed. Little did James know that their paths would cross under the most extraordinary of circumstances.

'Hi James, Max here, how are you?'

'Mr Gustav, long time no speak, how the devil are you old man?'

'I'm fine. May have a bit of business for you. Got a woman with early stage breast cancer who's got a benefactor. She may be interested in paying you a visit. Usual set up – I've told her she needs the most advanced treatment which we can't accommodate here so she'll have to pay more by going to London. You see where I'm going with this?'

'Of course, we split the profit fifty fifty. I'll need to assess the situation, of course, - don't want her thinking she's getting the inferior treatment so I'll have to work out the arrangements. What did you tell her about cost?

'£150 standard £285 specialised.'

'Nice one. That gives me room for manoeuvre. Where does she come from?'

'Lives in Cairo but comes from the Sudan.'

'Speaks English?'

'Yes.'

'Shame. You can get away with more if they don't speak the lingo'.

'Now now, don't be greedy James. I'll give you the details when she confirms.'

'You sound very confident Maxi boy.'

'I told her the chances of survival improved by 25% if she goes to London.'

'What bullshit. Happy days. I'll wait for your confirmation.'

CHAPTER FIVE

Rania told the Inspector that he had to be quick as she had to get back to her office. She'd already been missing for more than an hour and her absence would provoke gossip – especially as everybody thought she was having an affair with Errol Flynn. She took him to a small office on the ground floor which was used as a store room as well as a place for staff to get a bit of peace and quiet. She sat down on a swivel chair behind a desk and motioned him towards a small sofa by a bookcase on the far wall.

'How can I help you Inspector?'

Inspector Francis decided to 'go for the jugular':

'Did you murder Sir Michael Wilkinson?'

Rania was taken aback but didn't panic.

'Of course not' she said calmly. 'The case has been dropped and you have no jurisdiction to examine me on this matter so I suggest you stop before I phone the police.'

'I am the police.'

'You should know better then. I would quit while you're ahead Inspector because I'd hate to see you on a harassment charge which, if you continue, would be the result.'

'But it's your word against mine' said the Inspector. 'Besides, I'm on your side. I don't want to cause problems. I figured that MI5 had something to do with the murder of Dr Rob Williams so what you did was justified.'

'But I didn't do anything. More to the point the case has been dropped and you're out of order.'

'I know I am but things just don't stack up and I'm the sort of guy that gets restless if things don't make sense. The way I see it is this: You became attached to the doctor in Baghdad. Both of you were being spied upon either by the CIA or MI5 or both. He was vocal about his opposition to the war having discovered no evidence of weapons of mass destruction. He went back to London. You got a job in Cairo. You were followed and harassed by a contractor probably working for the CIA. This prompted the doctor to return to the Middle East in an attempt to protect you. Instead he got shot. An MI5 operative was sent out to kill the contractor as the latter knew too much. This operative was having an affair with Sir Michael and carried a photograph of him. Sir Michael, a happily married man, wanted this operative out the way. She ended up dead and the photograph was handed to the Cairo Police. The guy in charge was an Inspector Othman. His picture was all over the papers and confirmed that this was the Othman I knew and loved. We were best friends at university and have followed similar paths. Now I know Othman very well. He's a principled man, very clever and slightly mischievous. Do you know what I mean Rania?'

'I don't know what you're talking about.'

'I think you do. You see he gave you that photo so that you could exact revenge on your lover's killer – Sir Michael Wilkinson, Head of MI5. Knowing Othman, he'd probably provided you with the gun which you used to shoot him. I don't know how you got the gun through customs, if it was the gun he gave you, but, fair play, you did it. Othman got the glory for arresting the contractor who killed the MI5 operative and other people on the way, but he knew MI5 were behind the doctor's killing. Now, Othman's very much Old Testament – an eye for an eye and all that biblical stuff. On the other hand he wouldn't want to be associated with the assassination of the Head of MI5 – no way. So he got you, effectively, to do the dirty work. You could identify Sir Michael because you had the photograph – you could've identified him without this but the photograph makes the whole thing a little more poignant. You pinned it to his jacket after you shot him which, in a sense, was the final act of revenge as his family would've been distraught about the fact that he'd been playing around. You made off with his chauffeur to Waterloo Station where you changed into western clothes and went about your business in the normal way. Simples. What's more, because Othman was involved, he was effectively your accessory to murder – that's the way I'm looking at it. So whether you both planned it or not, the two of you could be in a place where the 'sun don't shine.'

'You're forgetting one thing Inspector. There was insufficient evidence to prove that I was the assassin. The only witness couldn't make a positive identification, there were no finger prints and I had two credible alibis who confirmed that I was with them at the time of the murder. Your enquiries are going nowhere. The case has been dropped. Besides you can't try a person twice for the same crime.'

'So you're not denying it? - in any event you've not been tried. The Crown Prosecution threw the case out. I reckon the police did a bad job. They never followed up on the photograph and, let's face it, you had a great motive for killing Sir Michael. The alibis were not properly scrutinized and the whole thing stinks. My story makes sense and the only thing you're saying is that there is insufficient evidence to prove the case beyond reasonable doubt. You know something Rania, I think the government and the rest of the authorities, including the police, were quite happy that Sir Michael was dealt with because it kind of takes the limelight off them. Sir Michael would've been given the nod from someone in government to silence the doctor and he together with the CIA took this literally and had him knocked off. With Sir Michael dead, the government's hoping that's the end of the matter. What do you think?'

'All conjecture and all too late. Goodbye Inspector.'

'There's just one thing Rania.'

'What's that?'

'Despite everything, a murder was committed and they still haven't found the murderer.'

'So?'

'Well, we do have the best judicial system in the world and justice must be seen to be done.'

'What are you getting at?'

'It's obvious. The public want crimes to be solved. This one hasn't and all it takes is a few words to the right newspapers for the whole case to be resurrected.'

'And who's going to the newspapers?'

'For a small fee, I'll keep my mouth shut.'

'That's blackmail.'

'At last, we have an understanding. Goodbye Ms Hakim.'

CHAPTER SIX

Mohammed reached for his phone and di-alled the number Othman had given him. He explained that they had visited Mr Gustav at the private clinic and that the diagnosis was worse than they had expected. Magda's best chance of survival was to travel to London to receive special-ised treatment but this would cost nearly £300,000. Othman said he would find a way and suggested both families rallied to raise the funds. He had connections in both the Egyptian and UK govern-ments having become somewhat of a hero in track-ing down and arresting the murderer of the MI5 operative. He may be able to negotiate a loan, or even a grant, to supplement the funds generated by both families.

It was agreed that Mohammed and Magda would pay for the flights and accommodation having saved a tidy amount over the years through the profits from their launderette. The families and, hopefully, respective governments, would pay for the rest. Othman told Mohammed to confirm the situation with Mr Gustav and get on the first available flight to the UK. He would put them up in a hotel on a temporary basis.

Magda contacted her sister who was more than happy to look after her two children and started packing the cases. Mohammed notified Mr Gustav that they wished to travel to London and gave him the details of their benefactor. Gustav warned Mohammed that Mr Nathan would need a deposit so he had better prepare accordingly. He advised him to phone the hospital as soon as he'd settled in London. After he'd finished giving all the relevant details he phoned Nathan:

'Hi James, the fishes are hooked.'

'Good man. When are they coming over?'

'Within the next few days. I told them that you would need a deposit. I'll send you their details and her medical records. I 'll assume you'll get them to sign the agreement once you've seen them?'

'No problem'.

Meanwhile Mohammed looked around their small living room. Magda was sitting by the window staring at the small garden. It wasn't really a garden, more a courtyard with a couple of shrubs and bushes sprouting from spaces made in the concrete floor. A palm tree stood in the corner with its rugged palms swaying in the gentle breeze. Behind the palm tree a white wall provided a temporary home for two small lizards who'd decided to sun bathe rather than scamper around looking for small insects in the mid day heat. Time stood still as the two lizards contemplated their next moves. Inside, the small room needed decorating. The plaster was flaky in places and missing altogether in other parts revealing ancient red bricks which, presumably, held the building together. In the middle of the stone floor was a withered old rug showing what would have been a line of camels carrying their produce across the Sahara. The picture had faded over time preventing a clear view of the forms which had been carefully woven many years ago. A table and four chairs were positioned to the side of the room while, on the other stood an old cooker which had served the family for over 20 years. A few books lay on shelves in the alcoves and facing the large window at the back of the room was a thread bare sofa the covering of which had seen better days. Magda sat on this sofa and stared into nothingness. The room was gloomy and still. Only the rustling of the palms could be heard as the light dimmed and shadows cast mysterious shapes on the white walls. The silence hung like a huge weight which was impossible to lift. The kids were upstairs and had been told of the plans. They accepted the situation with solemn resignation and threw themselves into study. Only the parakeets broke the silence as they flew wildly through the trees making their screeching sounds. At last Mohammed spoke:

'We've got to look on the positive side my dear. We must have hope. The good news is that the cancer is treatable. Even better, you're going to get the best treatment in the world. I've heard that Mr Nathan is renowned for his expertise and has all the knowledge needed to administer the new technology. We must be thankful to Othman and our families. But most of all we must thank Allah. We are in his hands – whatever will be will be. We must trust in him for your full recovery my love.'

'I know Mohammed but I'm scared. I'm scared of so many things. Leaving the children, leaving Cairo, flying to London, meeting new people – it's all too much. May Allah give me strength.'

'He will, he will. Just trust in him and things will be fine inshallah.'

CHAPTER SEVEN

Rania and the mad professor mingled with the crowd at the exhibition and offered information to anyone who looked like they were on the verge of asking a question. The professor was a natural exhibitionist and dramatically explained the origins of the figures without much prompting from the punters. To some he presented as a stage performer and they were embarrassed by his antics. To others he was an intelligent entertainer and they listened intently to what he had to say with a gaze in their eyes which suggested an admiration which bordered on worship. Rania, on the other hand, was more reserved and, some would say, more 'normal' in her dealings with the public. She exuded a confidence and displayed an intellect which, in a sense, when combined, resulted in a more credible performance than that of the great thespian professor (who had, by this time, selected the more attractive members of his audience for special praise, subjecting them to his irresistible wit and romantic catch phrases – some of which proved to be inappropriate).

Rania checked her watch amidst the relative chaos and reminded herself that she was meeting Othman in five minutes time. She caught the professor's attention and pointed to her watch. He acknowledged her concern and motioned her to go. He would take a later lunch. Besides, he was enjoying himself to such a degree, especially with one American woman, that he put the thought of a break to the back of his mind – he had conquests to make!

Rania ran to the ladies and looked at herself in the mirror. She wasn't sure why men found her attractive. He nose was a little big and slightly hooked and her mouth was uneven. On the other hand her eyes were dark and piercing and her teeth were straight and brilliantly white. Once the eye make-up and lipstick had been applied, her smile facilitated a facial transition from ordinary to stunning. A shake of the head loosened her long black hair, with a wisp falling over her forehead, transforming the image, once again, to that of tantalising beauty. Add this to the fact that she was tall, lean and curvy and the picture of Cleopatra – a renowned Egyptian beauty as projected by Elizabeth Taylor – springs to mind. On the other hand Rania was very modest, probably due to her Muslim upbringing, and did not regard herself as beautiful or even attractive. She did not have regular features and thought herself to be quite plain. This, of course, added to her attractiveness as most intelligent men don't normally like women who are so obviously aware of their beauty and flaunt their wares at every opportunity. Anyway, she finished doing her make- up, brushed her hair again and made her way to the exit. She got to the top of the steps and saw Othman leaning against the railings at the entrance of the museum. She waved and he waved back. They met half way up the steps and he kissed her cheeks and held her hand.

'Great to see you again Rania' he said.

'It's been a long time' she said. 'How are you, what have you been doing and how long are you over here?'

'Let's find a place we can talk. I think I'm going to be here for some time.'

'Okay, I know a place round the corner. It's a small hotel and we should be able to find a quiet place to talk.'

They found a table in the small foyer by the window and ordered coffee. The hotel had not been decorated for some time. The carpet was old and the floral wallpaper was yellow with age and cigarette smoke. The table and chairs had been stained dark oak and the reception desk needed desperate re-staining to cover the damage caused by wear and tear. But the hotel was cosy. An old fashion fireplace dominated one side of the room and a coal fire was burning which reminded Othman of the one Dickens novel he had read – 'Pickwick Papers' – many years ago and after several attempts.

'Right Rania, tell me all?'

'Okay, but before I give you my life story from the moment I left Cairo, I must share something with you.'

'What's that?'

'Do you now a guy called Nigel Francis?'

'Why yes. We were great friends at university. He joined the police the same time as I did. How on earth did you come across his name?'

'I've done more than that. I met him yesterday. He's been following Rob's case and has convinced himself that I killed Wilkinson.'

'And what did you say?'

'I denied it. More to the point I've been eliminated from enquiries. The case has been dropped.'

'Did you kill him?'

'That's not the issue. The problem is this: your friend doesn't think the police did a very good job in presenting their case to the CPS and wants to go to the newspapers to resurrect the case against me.'

'He can't do that. The case against you is finished.'

'Othman, this is the free world, not the Middle East. Anything goes in exposing the truth.'

'And what is the truth Rania?'

'You're missing the point. He knows that you were involved in the investigations and has put two and two together to establish that you gave me the photograph of Wilkinson which, in fairness, you did. He also reckons you provided me with the gun that shot him. From his analysis all fingers point to me as the assassin. However, his thinking is that since you provided the photograph and the gun, you are also implicated.'

'Yes but you and I know that MI5, the CIA and the British government were behind Rob's killing. The murder of Wilkinson has done everybody a favour.'

'I know that but, at the moment, there is no proof that these authorities were linked to Rob's killing. Besides, Nigel's angle is that, despite all the cover ups, there's still a murderer out there on the run. He tells me that in this country, no matter what the background or circumstances, justice must be seen to be done and, at the moment, the case of Wilkinson's murder has yet to be solved. He reckons that with a bit more research he could make the headlines – with me and you highlighted in the tabloids.'

'So what. Surely we just do nothing. I'll have a word with him. I'm sure we can sort this out. Nigel is a great guy. Once he knows the full background, he'll drop it'.

'I'm not so sure that he's such a great guy. He may have changed since you knew him.'

'How come?'

'If I don't confess to the murder, he will black-mail me. In other words I pay him to keep me and you out the press. That's the way I see it.'

'Has he said this?'

'More or less. Enough to put the frighteners on me.'

'This really doesn't sound like Nigel. On one hand he talks about justice, on the other he talks about blackmailing you. He was a man of principle. I wonder what's happened to him?'

'I don't know but he's not going to let this one rest.'

'Look Rania, I trust you and believe what you've told me. I'm in this as much as you are. Yes I gave you the photograph as a prompt to get to the truth. Yes I gave you a gun which you may or may not have used. But I could argue that I never meant you to kill Wilkinson. I could also argue that I gave you a gun strictly for self defence purposes as you were not safe in Cairo. You could argue it the other way saying I'd given you these things for the sole purpose of eliminating Wilkinson. We've got to work together on this and be honest with each other. I'm going to assume that you did kill Wilkinson. If I'm right, nod your head.'

'I don't need to nod my head Othman. I did kill that bastard but didn't use the gun you gave me. I left that in Cairo. Instead I paid someone to get me a gun when I arrived in the UK.'

'Who?'

'A friend of the local Imam who happened to be the secretary of a country shooting club. A very respectable man working in the city and a devout Muslim.'

'Where's this gun now.'

'In a box under the floorboards under my bed.'

'Okay Rania, leave this to me. Let me speak to Nigel. I can check his whereabouts at the local police station although doubtless he'll be making contact with you soon.'

'Thanks, now let's talk about you. Why are you here?'

'To see you and also to help a Sudanese friend who needs specialised cancer treatment in London. She should be flying over from Cairo as we speak. I promised to help her and her husband with the expenses including accommodation. They were very helpful to me in Rob's case and I owe them.'

'You're like Rob, always the man of principle.'

'Change that to some principle. I'm not squeaky clean.'

'None of us are Othman. Keep in touch. You've got my mobile. I'll let you know if I get another visit from your friend. Hopefully, you'll make contact with him before he gets to me.'

'I'll try. Speak soon.'

They drank their coffee, kissed and left. Rania back to the museum. Othman back to his hotel.

CHAPTER EIGHT

I t was the 5th July 2004 and Othman was making his way to Gatwick Airport to pick up Mohammed and Magda. They had never been to the UK before or, indeed, anywhere in Europe or the States, so he was anxious to help them adapt to a new culture. Fortunately, both of them were well educated and could speak good English so he didn't believe there would be too much of a problem.

He'd hired a Ford Galaxy which would be big enough to accommodate their luggage – he doubted whether they would bring much - Mohammed and Magda were very resourceful people and could always make the best out of very little. It followed, in his mind, bearing in mind this trait, that they would bring the essentials, and not much else. He hoped he hadn't got this wrong and they wouldn't be bringing the kitchen sink!

The journey was arduous going through London but improved greatly when he hit the A3 at Wandsworth. As he travelled south towards the M25 he noticed how the scenery changed. There weren't so many houses or buildings; there were more open spaces; more trees and more fields. When he arrived at the top of the M23 there was hardly a building in site and the landscape was decidedly hilly, probably the beginnings of the North Downs which continued eastwards towards Maidstone. After about fifteen minutes he arrived at Gatwick and parked his car. He made his way to arrivals and checked the board for delays. Their flight was on time which meant they had arrived and were collecting their cases. He'd better not have a coffee as they might come through customs at any time and didn't want them to panic unnecessarily as they entered the manic concourse.

At last, two worried faces appeared from the duty free shop and hesitantly made their way to where Othman was standing. He rushed up to them and took hold of their two suitcases and guided them towards a seat. They both sat down with a sigh of relief feeling as though they'd been through a war zone.

'Hi Othman' Mohammed said 'We made it!'

'Of course you did, let's get you into the car. Do you think you can manage a short walk?'

'Lead the way' Magda said as she got up from her seat. 'After that flight, a short walk seems like heaven. I've never been through so much turbulence.'

'I didn't know you'd flown before?'

'Only internal flights from Cairo to Khartoum, nothing like we've just experienced.'

'Okay, well. You've made it now so just relax. Soon you'll be in a comfy hotel.'

They made their way to the car park and let Othman carry their cases. He put them in the boot and Mohammed and Magda took their places in the back seat. Neither of them wished to sit in the front.

The drive back was uneventful apart from Mohammed's gasps at the politeness and orderly fashion of the British driving fraternity. He was used to shouting, horn blowing and tempers being lost in Cairo, while in Surrey all he experienced was a neat line of fast moving traffic with drivers focussed on their driving rather than shouting at each other through their opened windows. Magda noticed the green fields and, of course, the trees – so many different types. She now understood the song which included the line '...in England's green and pleasant land'. The countryside for her summed up this phrase written by the poet William Blake and put to music by Hubert Parry. She'd read about these people on

Wikipedia and the sentiment of the poem had stuck in her mind. She'd always wanted see this 'green and pleasant land', but not under these circumstances where her life was threatened by a horrible disease.

When they entered London Othman took them on the road which gave them a good view of the Houses of Parliament. He then went over Waterloo Bridge and told them to look out on both sides. They sat there in amazement. The architecture was so different to what they had been used to in Cairo. Buildings had been completed; there was no litter (as far as they could see); the roads were straight and distinct; the layout of the city was so structured, so organised and the buildings themselves so clean, so interesting and so diverse. Some were old, some were new. There were domes, crosses, spires, roofs, odd shapes, regular shapes – all, it seemed, in harmony with the vibrancy of the city. There were no street sellers or beggars or disabled people pleading for help. This truly was a great city and Magda, in awe of its greatness, expected to see 'streets paved with gold', although Mohammed reminded her that this was just a story and that she might just be pushing her imagination a little too far! Othman brought them down to reality and told them there were beggars, street sellers and disabled people around but they just weren't visible as they drove through the main streets.

They arrived at their hotel and Othman helped to register them at the front desk before taking their luggage to their room which was situated on the first floor. The first thing they did was to make a cup of tea.

'Right. First thing to do is to phone Nathan and make an appointment. The sooner we get your treatment started Magda the better. Both the UK and Egyptian governments will be making a contribution to the fees. In fact they have already credited my account, so please don't worry about the costs. What's important is to get you better. If you like I'll phone Nathan and get the ball rolling.'

'That would be great Othman. I don't know what we'd do without you' said Mohammed.

'No problem, I'll phone his secretary now. Have you got the papers?'

The papers consisted of a financial statement and contact numbers. The rest of the documents, including Magda's medical records, had been sent direct to Nathan.

'I wish to speak to Mr James Nathan, Senior Oncologist.'

'Who is this please?' asked his secretary.

'My name is Othman and I am the benefactor for Mrs Magda Ishmail.'

'Othman who?'

'Just Othman. My second name is also Othman.'

'So it's Othman Othman?'

''Yes, if you like, but I'm just known as Othman.'

'I'll put you through.'

There was a pause as the secretary wrestled with the new telephone system which had caused nothing but aggravation since its installation earlier in the year. At last, a voice spoke:

'Ah Mr Othman, how can I help?'

'Is that James Nathan?'

'It is.'

'Fine. Mrs Magda Ishmail and her husband Mohammed have just arrived in the UK and are anxious to see you.'

'Yes I have all the papers. I will need to see them as soon as possible to sign the agreement and to plan the next steps. It is crucial that we start treatment as soon as possible. However, I will need a £5000 deposit to initiate proceedings.'

'Of course Mr Nathan. I will prepare a cheque.'

'Fine, how about 10.30 am tomorrow?'

'We will be there. Is it the same address as shown on the financial statement?'

'Yes, that's right. See you tomorrow.'

Othman left the two of them in their hotel and promised to pick them up tomorrow at 9.30 am. They would have to take the underground which would be a new experience for them and one which they probably wouldn't enjoy. He had it in mind that after the first appointment he would leave them to it and concentrate on his other problem – Rania Hakim.

He didn't sleep very well that night. He kept tossing and turning, thinking of Rania and the potential mess she'd gotten herself into. Othman had rather hoped she would've found some other way to silence Wilkinson but, having thought that, he'd not dispelled the idea of his assassination, through the hands of Rania, at the time he'd handed her the photograph. Perhaps he'd got too big for his boots. Wanted all the glory but without the responsibility of another's murder. He hoped that he could appease his old chum Nigel. If he explained the whole situation to him he might just come round to thinking that Wilkinson's death was justified – on grounds of principle. Clearly in Egypt or any other Middle Eastern country such a murder, given all the circumstances, would've been categorised as an 'honour killing' and from this perspective, would've been justified. He wondered, however, whether the system in UK would allow for such an approach or whether the legal stance would be that all murders are unjustified, no matter what the circumstances or mitigating factors. He didn't know enough about English criminal law to conclude on the matter. Safe to say he was worried – not just for Rania but for himself. Had he overstepped the mark when he gave Rania the gun and photograph? Of course he had. He should not have given her the gun and should've given the photograph to the British Embassy. He'd played God and would now have to figure a way out of his dilemma.

Next day Othman met Mohammed and Magda outside Holborn Underground Station and accompanied them to Harley Street where Nathan conducted affairs from an office newly renovated to reflect his growing status among the oncology fraternity. The two of them were like ' rabbits caught in the headlights' as they moved with the crowd down the escalators on to the platform. They were used to crowds but not in such a confined space, several metres underground. They were astounded by the noise as the train approached the station – a whistling sound that got louder and louder until it burst into thunder as the train exited the tunnel – and held on to each other as the train slowed down, passing them on the way. They waited for the doors to open and, without thinking, tried to enter the carriage. This proved unsuccessful as a hoard of commuters rushed off the train and nearly flattened them in the process. They soon realised that it was best to let people off first before attempting to enter the carriage. Once inside they managed to find a corner and, squashed together, held on grimly to each other as the train got underway. The train was so packed they couldn't even see a seat let alone sit on one, and the people who got on and off looked so unfriendly, almost wild looking, moving frantically to find a space, or, if this were not possible, gently and subtly pushing other passengers to make room while apologising at the same time. All this time Othman grinned at their predicament. He knew they would be disconcerted by the whole underground experience, and he was not disappointed.

At last they arrived at Regent's Park Station and after several attempts at opening the turnstiles with their oyster cards, found themselves looking at the railings surrounding Regent's Park. After a short walk they located Nathan's offices and Othman registered them in the reception area. They sat down on leather sofas and waited. Magda was getting used to the waiting and resigned herself to fate and, indeed, the will of Allah.

After only a few minutes a very attractive young girl walked into the room, introduced herself as Mr Nathan's secretary and invited them to follow her. They walked down a short corridor until they reached Mr Nathan's office. She knocked and then opened the door: They were greeted by a stocky red-face man:

'Ah, Mr and Mrs Ishmail I presume, and you sir are?'

'Othman, Chief Inspector Othman.'

'Come to check on me Chief Inspector?' Nathan joked.

'Of course not, I'm a close friend and benefactor.'

'Good, good, good, now come in and sit down. Tea or coffee?'

Mr James Nathan was in his thirties or forties, completely bald with a designer beard which he'd shaven the night before. His ears indicated a rugby background; big and misshapen, but his hands indicated a more delicate past time – perhaps music or even, although it seemed unlikely, embroidery.

'No thank you ' they all said.

'Right, let's get down to business. I've seen your records and results Mrs Ishmail and I'm satisfied that you have a more advanced and aggressive breast cancer which, I assure you, is treatable. It's an unusual kind of tumour but, with our advanced technology, I'm sure we can tackle it. Of course, I want to give you some more tests and have booked you in this afternoon for an MRI, various other scans and a visit to the pathology department. Is that Okay with you?'

'Of course Mr Nathan' said Magda.

'Good, good, good. I need you to sign a few forms which firstly notify you of the treatment programme and secondly asks for your written consent. The other forms constitute an agreement of the same, including the costs, the liability for the costs and the details of your benefactor. My secretary normally deals with the paperwork but on this occasion I'm going to handle such matters

– I want to make sure that everything's right. It's all self explanatory and I'll give you a few moments to complete the documents. Meanwhile, do you think you can give us a specimen of your urine and stools Mrs Ishmail?'

Magda was a bit shocked.'I'll try' she said.

'Good. My assistant will help you if you go into that room. Now, gentleman, I'll leave you to read and complete the documents and I'll be back in about 20 minutes. Is that okay?'

'Fine.'

Nathan finally returned, made himself a cup of coffee and asked his assistant how Magda was doing. It had been a success so the containers were sent down to the path lab for a quick analysis. After about fifteen minutes he got a call from one of the technicians which he decided to take in the reception area. The technician confirmed that both specimens were clear. He went back to his office and saw the three of them huddled round his desk busy signing the forms.

'Okay. Do you understand everything? If so I want you Mrs Ishmail to start chemotherapy tomorrow morning at the UCH hospital. I've already booked you an appointment for 9.30 a.m. Mr Othman, if you could give me a cheque for £5000 we're all done here. Oh, one last thing, I'm afraid they found traces of blood in your urine and stools Mrs Ishmail. Nothing to worry about. We'll just upgrade the chemo to make sure we give you a proper clear out. This thing is quite normal, you know and, as I said, nothing to worry about.'

There was no real reason for asking for a stool specimen but Nathan thought it would add more credibility to his investigations and resultant treatment.

'Fine' said Magda 'Can we go now, I feel very tired.'

Nathan collected the signed forms and cheque and bid them farewell. Othman didn't say anything apart from pointing out the nearest station to the UCH. He left them at their hotel and told them he'd keep in touch, although he had other business to attend to. They thanked him profusely and went up to their room to prepare for the afternoon's appointment. Othman thought about Nathan. His manner had been too abrupt, too confident. He didn't trust him although he daren't say anything. It may have been his normal way. Some doctors were not particularly friendly but were brilliant at what they did. Othman decided to park his thoughts, giving Nathan the benefit of the doubt - for the time being.

━⟨┼ ┼⟩━

Othman decided to pop in to the museum on his way home to see Rania and maybe have a look around.

His briefcase was checked by security at the entrance and he soon found himself in a large hall with a round structure in the middle. There were doors leading off the sides, which obviously led to the exhibits, and shops located at the base of the structure. He ambled through the shops, brought himself a coffee and used the loo. After that he found himself a seat, sat down and called Rania:

'Hi, what are you doing?'

'Working, where are you?'

'I'm sitting in the main hall, wondered if you were free for a chat?'

'Sure. Down in a minute.'

Othman gazed around the hall. It had been recently refurbished and he could smell the freshness of the paint as it dried on the walls. The place was packed with people from every part of the globe – there were school children, young people, old people, families, groups being led by guides and smiling officials who had clearly benefitted from some recent customer care training as they displayed over attentive behaviour towards the new arrivals.

'Hi there' Rania said as she parked herself next to Othman.

'Hi. How are you?'

'Fine. Any news?'

'No, I haven't tracked down Nigel yet but that's my next job.'

'Look Othman, I've got myself into this mess and I'm worried you're going to get too involved. Why don't you get the first plane back to Cairo and keep your head down. I was the one who decided on what I wanted to do, not you. You're the innocent party in all this and I don't see the point of you hanging around.'

'And leave you to the wolves of the media? No chance. I'm going to sort this out with Nigel one way or another. He'll listen to me. We go back a long way and I'm sure he's just bluffing.'

'I wish I shared your confidence' said Rania. 'I found him creepy like a snake. I wouldn't trust him.'

'But you don't know him like I do Rania. Let me speak with him first and then we can plan our next moves.'

'As I said before, he may have changed. So watch it'.

There was a pause in the conversation. Rania was just about to say something when they were confronted by the 'Nutty Professor.'

'And who is this my Egyptian beauty?' interrupted Professor Lear as he eyed Othman up and down.

'Oh hello professor, I'm Iraqi not Egyptian as you well know. May I introduce Othman. He's over here on holiday.'

'Delighted to meet you sir. Please call me Angus. That goes for you as well Rania so stop calling me professor. After all, we are intimate work colleagues.'

'Work colleagues yes, intimate no.' Rania laughed.

'Please to meet you Angus' said Othman.

The three of them wandered around the museum with Angus spouting off in his normal way and Rania rebuking him when she saw fit to do so. Othman for his part liked the professor and, despite his dramatic antics, believed he was a man that could be trusted. He had a genuine and credible manner. 'What you see is what you get' thought Othman in summarising the nature of the man, and, at the end of the day, on top off all this, Professor Angus Lear was hilariously funny – at least that's what Othman thought. Accordingly, they exchanged numbers, much to the secret disgust of Rania who thought Lear a liability.

The three of them spent some time examining ancient Egyptian relics and, despite the professor's intrusion into Othman's intended meeting with Rania, the time was well spent ending in an agreement that Rania and Othman would have dinner that night. The professor politely declined the offer despite the fact that none was made. Rania went back to work and Othman was just about to make his exit when the professor caught his arm:

'Can you hold on a minute?'

'Sure, how can I help?' Othman asked.

'Let's sit down here. I'm worried about Rania. I know she was suspected of killing the Head of MI5 because she told me. It's none of my business but Rania is a good worker and I don't like to see her upset.'

'Upset?'

'Yes. Something's wrong I can tell. Is she in trouble?'

'Not that I'm aware of. All charges were dropped so she's got nothing to worry about.'

'Maybe so, but something's not right. How do you know her?'

'We met in Cairo. She worked for the Cairo Museum and I worked for the police.'

'Can you tell me more?'

'There's nothing more to tell' Othman said, thinking on his feet. 'We met and became good friends. She wanted to travel and got herself a job here as you know. I stayed in Cairo and needed a holiday. I've got lots of contacts in the UK so decided to meet up with Rania. So here I am.'

'Right, well I care for Rania. She's a good person and wouldn't want to see her hurt. You say there's nothing wrong and I must accept your word. But if you need my help at any time, give me a call. You've got all my details.'

'Fine Angus, I'll bear that in mind. See you soon.'

CHAPTER NINE

I t was a clear afternoon as Othman made his way
down Theobalds Road towards the police station.
Things hadn't changed much in London since he'd
last been there. There was definitely more traffic
and people, and the pace was faster than he'd remembered. It was a more diverse city with just about
every nationality represented. What hadn't changed
was the weather – the grey clouds, the drizzle, the
dampness, the varying temperatures - all these
elements epitomised the UK's general climate and
wasn't about to change.

Othman entered the police station and asked the
sergeant on duty whether Inspector Nigel Francis

was around. He explained that he was an old university mate and was passing through London but didn't have any contact details. Othman was told to take a seat.

Nigel was told that a Mr Othman was downstairs claiming that they were old university buddies. He acted surprised but had an inkling he would be seeing Othman again, especially after his little chat with Rania Hakim. He went down to the reception area and prepared his opening words. He saw Othman sitting on one of the plastic chairs looking out through a window:

'Othman how are you?' Nigel approached him by playing a forward drive stroke with his imaginary cricket bat. 'Remember the good old days Othman – me starting the batting, taking on the onslaught with you coming in later to take all the glory? Those were the days. Now you're here and it's great to see you.'

'Great to see you Nigel.' They hugged and mockingly fought each other.

'We must have a pint. Have you got time?'

'Have you got time Nigel, you're on duty?'

'A swift pint won't hurt anybody. We can arrange dinner for a later date. I know a great pub near Holborn Circus. Quaint 16th century and all that. If we go now we might be able to secure the snug room.'

'You're on. Let's go.'

They walked down towards Holborn Circus discussing trivia and days gone by. Nigel had changed. He was more cynical, more homophobic and racist then he'd been before. He said the job had made him that way but behind it all he was the same old Nigel Francis. They entered an old ally way and after a few yards faced *Ye Olde Mitre* pub. As Nigel said, it was a typical 16th century establishment with panelled walls, open (gas) fire and historic pictures displayed in every 'nook and cranny'. On the left was a little room – the snug - which was empty. Nigel ordered two pints of bitter while Othman settled himself on the firm wooden bench.

'Cheers' Nigel said 'It's been a long time.'

'Too long' Othman replied.

'So what's brought you to Blightly?'

'A couple of reasons. First I wanted a break. You may have read in the newspapers that I was involved in the Dr Rob Williams case and, to be honest, after that caper I wanted a holiday.

'I had read about that – you got all the glory for capturing the murderer of the MI5 operative. I cut out the newspaper article. I said to myself – typical Othman, always gets the glory. What's the second reason?'

'I have a very close friend who's got breast cancer and wanted to get her the best treatment in

London. She's come over here with her husband and I'm looking after them. They're innocent Sudanese folk who've never stepped outside the Middle East so need their hands holding. I'm helping them with the finances as well.'

'How very gallant of you Othman. What's in it for you?'

'What do you mean?'

'I know you Othman. You're a very decent chap and all that but you can be, shall we say, a bit mischievous if you want something.'

'Not this time, I genuinely want to help them. I've got a bit of money saved up and with a little help from others, we've managed to raise some funds. She's evidently got an unusual cancer and London has better equipment then Cairo. Her best chance of a cure is right here. We're told her chances of survival are cut by 25% if she remained in Cairo. Anyway, I owe them. They were very helpful in the Rob Williams case.'

'Tell me more.'

'Can't Nigel, best not to know.'

'Okay, get the message.'

There was a pause in the conversation. Othman quickly prepared what he wanted to say about Rania.

'Look Nigel, there's another reason why I made contact with you. I would've done anyway, you know that, but something has happened which makes our meeting important.'

'What's that?'

'Rania Hakim.'

'The girl who was suspected of shooting Sir Michael Wilkinson?'

'You know who I mean Nigel, you've been talking to her.'

'Have I? Police business Othman so what's it got to do with you?'

'I'm a friend of Rania's and she's been through some tough times. She loved Rob Williams and saw him get killed by the contractor who went on to kill the MI5 operative, Katerine O'Reilly. The contractor was going to 'spill the beans' on MI5 but was shot by some girl he'd raped. You've read all the papers. You know the score.'

'So what?'

Well, this MI5 operative was having an affair with the Head of MI5, Sir Michael Wilkinson and had been appointed by him to get rid of Williams through the contractor... at least that's what I think.'

'You're kidding me.'

'No I'm not. The contractor was blabbing too much after the murder so the operative was sent out to silence him. She failed but was left for dead. She had a photograph of her lover boy which happened to be Sir Michael.'

'All a bit far-fetched Othman.'

'I'm telling you the truth. You know me from old Nigel, I don't lie about things like this.'

'True.'

'Anyway, as far as I'm concerned, there's no question about MI5's involvement in the demise of Williams. You have to believe me on this one Nigel. I knew the UK government would deny their involvement and the whole thing would be covered up. My job in Cairo was done. I'd captured the assassin and there was no more I could do, apart, that is, from the photograph which tied Williams death to MI5.'

'You've lost me.'

'Look, the contractor told me his contact and paymaster was this MI5 operative, Katerine O'Reilly. She had identification papers which confirmed her background. Why should he lie about this? She came to kill him – why would he want to protect MI5's anonymity after an attempt on his life? Had he not been killed he would've disclosed his contacts thinking, if he did, he would be let off. He'd committed other crimes of course and disclosure may have given him his freedom pass. The fact that the operative appointed to silence Williams had a photograph with a love message written by the Head of MI5 confirmed to me that MI5 were behind the Williams killing.'

'So what did you do?'

'I gave the photograph to Rania.'

'Why?'

'I don't know. On one hand I was hoping she would use this as evidence and force the government to open an enquiry. On the other, I was hoping she would kill him.'

'Which she did?'

'Yes, for good reason.'

'I doubt the courts would look at it in that way.'

'No but the case has been dropped and I'm begging you not to go to the press. Rania has told me you're blackmailing her?'

The mood changed. Nigel sat there with his pint with a smug look on his face.

'I don't have to tell you this is Britain not Egypt. You might look at it as an 'honour killing' but in my book this was plain murder without justification. What's more Othman, by what you've told me, you're implicated. I can't keep quiet knowing there's a murderer on the loose. On the other hand, you're an old mate and I believe everything you've told me. As I said to Rania, I'm prepared to keep quiet for a fee. You said you were financing your friend's cancer treatment. If you're that rich you must be able to throw some cash my way.'

'You've changed Nigel. Rania was right. Look don't you see, MI5 were responsible for Dr Rob Williams assassination. What's more they got away with it. Sir Michael Wilkinson got his just desserts. Justice has been done.'

'That may be the case where your people come from but it's different over here. I'm giving you a chance to keep your career intact. Either you pay me or Rania pays, I don't care which. You got yourself into this mess but I'm quite happy to see you go back to Cairo in one piece. Rania's different. She's a killer and has to be dealt with.'

'How much do you want?'

'I'm a reasonable man Othman, as you know. 50k should do it. We'll meet here this time next week when you can hand me the cash in an envelope. No show means press releases in all the papers, believe me.'

'I thought you were my friend Nigel. I thought I could trust you.'

'Things have changed. We have to look after our own. Rania came over here, got herself a job and then murdered the Head of MI5. I don't care about the circumstances or whether it was justified or not – a murder is a murder, so you can forget about your old testament morals, they don't work anymore. Now pay up or suffer the consequences.'

'I'm not playing your corrupt games. You're supposed to be a cop and cops don't blackmail people. You've let your profession down and I might just decide to go to the complaints authorities.'

'Be my guest Othman. Think about your predicament man. Do the right thing. I'll see you next week.'

With that Nigel got up and left leaving Othman to his unfinished beer. He sat there for a few moments. He was in shock. He couldn't believe what his old buddy had said. He'd become cynical, twisted and greedy. What had made him change? He pondered on the situation. He was not going to be blackmailed by anyone so the option of paying Nigel 50K was a non-starter. He could take the next flight to Cairo and keep his head down, but that wasn't his style. He wanted to face the music, no matter what. That left the doing nothing option which risked Nigel carrying out his threat. So what could he reveal to the papers? He pictured a press release:

NEW EVIDENCE IN THE MI5 KILLING

Nigel Francis, an experienced Metropolitan Police Inspector, claims that he has found new evidence in relation to the Head of MI5 murder. Sir Michael Wilkinson was shot in the chest on 29th May 2003 by an unidentified person thought to be a woman. The murderer has never been found although, Inspector Francis believes that, whoever killed Sir Michael had been given a photograph from an Inspector who was conducting enquiries following the death of Dr Rob Williams. This photograph was found pinned to Sir Michael's jacket.

The Inspector is requesting the Home Office to sanction a resurrection of this case so that further investigations can be undertaken.

This is all the papers could say at this point as the case against Rania had been dropped and the case could not be resurrected until Home Office clearance had been secured. Othman felt confident. He would do nothing for the time being. Even if the case were resurrected he could admit to giving Rania the photograph but could deny that he suggested she killed the Head of MI5. The truth is he didn't and knowing Rania she would corroborate his evidence. The questions for him would be why did he give her the photograph, what was his motive and was his motive credible? It could still get messy and he cursed the day he'd handed her the picture. Meanwhile he would not be blackmailed and decided to sit it out.

Inspector Nigel Francis got back to his office, sat in his chair with his feet up on his desk and played back the recordings he'd made of the conversations he'd had with Rania and Othman. 'I think the Home Office will be interested in these tapes' he told himself.

That evening Othman met Rania in a Lebanese restaurant off the Edgware Road. She was looking beautiful as usual in a blue blouse and tight fitting black trousers. Her black hair was flowing down her back with a curl falling down over her forehead. Her eyes were a piercing blue made even more stunning by the use of make-up. Her figure was lean but curvy suggesting a rigorous routine at the gym, probably twice a day. Othman, like any man, could easily fall for her but he held back. At the end of the day she'd murdered Sir Michael. She may have got away with it in the Middle East on the grounds that the killing was justified but over here the situation was different.

The restaurant was busy but they found themselves a corner at the back where there was a good chance they could have a quiet conversation without interruption. Othman explained to her that he'd seen Nigel and that he wanted 50K to keep quiet:

'What?' Rania cried.

'Keep your voice down Rania, yes 50K, otherwise he'll go to the press and apply to the Home Office for a resurrection of the case – against you.'

'But Sir Michael deserved to die, not only did he arrange for Rob to be killed but he was having a sordid affair at the same time.'

'I know that, but as Nigel pointed out, this is not the Middle East. There are different values here and we've got to play by the rules. Besides, the government will find a way through their lawyers to cast doubt on any connection they may have had with Dr Williams. The fact is you have admitted to me that you did kill Sir Michael and I'm implicated because I provided you with his photograph. I may not have told you to kill him but my motives will be scrutinized and I'm likely to suffer career wise at the very least.'

'So what do we do?'

'I'm not paying him a penny and nor should you. Nigel has changed, you were right. He's in it for the money and his principles have flown out the window. I think we should call his bluff. Let's wait and see. He'll have to get Home Office approval and, in the meantime, any newspaper headline will have to be bland otherwise specific disclosures would taint the Office's decision. Whatever happens, my guess is that the process will take a long time. Also, we have some ace cards up our sleeves. For a start, the case was dropped against you and Nigel is going to have to present a pretty robust argument if he is to have any chance of Home Office approval. Secondly, you could not be identified and although the photograph does point the finger, the case has to be proven beyond all reasonable doubt.'

'What exactly does that mean?'

'Well, even if I admitted giving you the photograph that doesn't automatically mean that you killed Sir Michael. You may have given the photo to someone else or you may have simply lost it. Also you have two alibis who have already vouched that you were with them at the time of the killing. If they've lied once they will be under extreme pressure to lie again – on your behalf. Having said all that, your strongest evidence is that you were not caught in the act – no one can identify who the killer was. So, you see, the case for the prosecution is not going to be straight forward – there has to be no doubt.'

'But I don't like all this lying. I didn't give the photo to anyone else and I didn't lose it. The other thing, of course, is that I don't want my alibis to be dragged into my affairs again. God knows how they'd perform under cross examination.'

'I can understand that. But I still think we should stay calm and sit it out. I don't think the UK government will want this case to be resurrected because it will bring up the Rob Williams case again. The powers that be will not want that. They want this whole thing dead and buried, I'm sure of it.'

'That's all very well, but how long will this thing hang over our heads. We can't get on with our lives with this guy Nigel Francis making all kinds of threats'.

'Look Rania, even if we pay him, he may still carry out his threats. He's changed and I don't trust him. We should do nothing and wait. If he visits you, continue to deny everything. I have to tell you that because I thought Nigel would be on our side I told him everything – I told him that I gave you Sir Michael's photograph and told him that you admitted to me that you killed him. You could say that I've got it wrong and that none of these things happened. You could say that we don't get on because you rejected my advances and I decided to make up lies against you in revenge. Use your imagination but make sure you deny everything and don't make any offers to him'

'I'm not happy about any of this. Maybe I should just face the music. Perhaps after the public have heard the whole story they'll be sympathetic and I'll get off lightly?'

'I don't know Rania. Maybe, maybe not. But at the moment do nothing. Trust me, let's wait and see what happens.'

CHAPTER TEN

The UCH waiting room for patients receiving chemotherapy is not a happy place. It is large, modern and impersonal. Despite the nurses, doctors and support staff all having big smiles on their faces the atmosphere cannot but help reflect the fears and anxieties of the patients and their loved ones as they wait to be called.

Magda and Mohammed were no exceptions. They sat there hand in hand waiting for Magda's name to be announced as she shivered at the prospect of having poisonous drugs pumped into her blood stream. After so many years of research, the medical profession were still unable to find a treatment less barbaric. Surely a simple vaccine like small pox was the answer?

Mohammed surveyed the faces around the waiting room. Some were smiling, some were reading some were anxious and some looked terrified. There were just as many young people as old which may have reflected the fact that many cancers were picked up at an early stage rather than in the later stages. Unfortunately cancer does not discriminate, it doesn't select its victims: everybody – black, white, young old, male, female - can be affected. On that cheery note a nurse announced the name of Magda Ishmail and the two of them made their way to the treatment room.

The room was sterile. There were individual areas surrounded by curtains with people sitting with intravenous needles stuck in their hands reading magazines or talking to their companions about trivia. There were others sitting alone waiting for the effects of the drug to take hold and wishing they hadn't bothered their GP with the small mole they discovered some weeks ago. Others were smiling with an inane look on their faces as if to say – 'this should never have happened, I shouldn't be sitting here.'

Magda was led to her chair and the nurse brought up the apparatus. She was just about to talk to Magda when James Nathan, Senior Oncologist entered the room.

'Ah, Mr and Mrs Ishmail. How are you both? Or is that a bit of a stupid question?'

'We're fine 'said Mohammed putting on a brave face.

'Now look here, the both of you, you are in very good hands. Aren't they nurse?'

'The best' she said.

'Now, I'm starting you off with a drug known as Taxotere. We'll see how you get on with this treatment and review the situation in two weeks time. You may experience tiredness, sickness and hair loss but this is very common and there's nothing to worry about. Over to you nurse.'

'Wait a minute Mr Nathan, we were told there would be hardly any side effects' said Mohammed.

'There are always side effects Mr Ishmail and, of course, each patient is different so we can never be sure of the impact treatments of this kind have on each individual. You do understand?'

'I suppose so.'

Nathan left the treatment room leaving the nurse to set up the drip. Magda closed her eyes and held Mohammed's hand so tightly that her veins began to show.

'Good' said the nurse 'I can use that hand if you don't mind Mrs Ishmail. The veins are very clear which will cause less discomfort.'

The nurse found a suitable vein and gently pushed the needle into the heart of it. It was uncomfortable for Magda and she winced as the needle was pushed in further.

'That's it, we're there. Right, let's start fighting this cancer' she said as she released the drug into Magda's body.

The two of them sat there staring at each other, waiting for something to happen. But nothing did. Magda overcame the initial shock of the needle and felt no changes to her body. They talked about trivial things – what they would do for the remainder of the day, what would Othman be doing, would their children be okay, what a nice man Mr Nathan was – and looked around the treatment room to see others in the same predicament. This would be their life for the next few months so they had better get used to it –these were the thoughts going through both their minds.

CHAPTER ELEVEN

Inspector Nigel Francis did not hear from Othman and so decided to call him. It had been nearly two weeks and nothing had happened. He rang his mobile. Othman told him that he would not be meeting him at the pub and would certainly not be paying him any money. The tone of his voice indicated that their friendship was over. Nigel warned him of the consequences and was told to go to hell.

Later that morning he found himself in front of the Deputy Chief Constable of the Metropolitan Police. A weedy looking man with a receding hairline and glasses that looked too big for him. His name was Richard Scott, a graduate who had moved fast up the ranks through political scheming, careful manoeuvring and an ability to avoid blame. He'd experienced little front line action but because he presented as an intellectual – full of jargon and blue sky theories - the powers that be decided he would make a good leader. How wrong were they! Richard Scott was an abdicator rather than a delegator. Whenever there was a problem, it was never his fault despite his authoritative position. It was always someone else – never him. Consequently, he was no leader at all, just a clever bureaucrat. He was the same age as Nigel and they had known each other for many years. Both held senior positions in the masons and both liked a drink!

'So what have you got for me Nigel?'

'Good morning Richard, do you remember the MI5 case?'

'What the murder of Sir Michael Wilkinson?'

'That's right.'

'Go on.'

'Well if you remember a Ms Rania Hakim was the chief suspect but CPS threw it out.'

'I remember.'

'I saw her the other day and had a chat.'

'Why?'

'Out of curiosity. You see whoever killed Sir Michael pinned a photograph with a love message on his jacket.'

'Not necessarily.'

'Ah but all fingers point, Richard. Anyway to cut a long story short, she was tangled up in the Dr Rob Williams case in Cairo and the Inspector involved, Othman, who I know from university days, has disclosed to me that he did give the photograph in question to Rania and that she confessed to him that she'd killed Sir Michael. With this evidence, I'm sure she'd break under cross examination'

'What evidence?'

Nigel played both recordings back to Richard who, without warning, became extremely excited, springing from his chair like some scared gazelle and then grinning like some hyena who was just about to eat his prey.

'Oh this is good. This is very good. It doesn't really prove much but it's worth pursuing. This could look good for both of us Nigel. Tell me more.'

'Well, as you can see, Rania denied everything. The interesting thing was that she just relied on her alibis and the fact that she was not identified. She didn't deny that she received the photograph from Othman, nor deny that she murdered Sir Michael. She kept off these subjects. She was hoping that as the case was dropped, the police could do nothing more. I then met Othman down the pub. He's over here with some friends. We go back a long way and he was hoping, if he told me everything, I would forget about the whole thing. He kept going on about the government being behind the Dr Rob Williams murder and that Sir Michael's killing was justified. I reminded him that this wasn't the Middle East and that murder was murder no matter how much you dressed it up. What both of them didn't know was that I was secretly recording everything they said.'

'I don't know whether that evidence will be admissible but it's enough to get the ball rolling. You get on to the papers Nigel, I'll have a word with the Home Secretary. Don't go telling the chief, I want the glory on this one. I'll just say that we didn't have time to involve him as he wasn't around and thought we were doing the right thing. His days are numbered in any case. Now hand me over a copy of those recordings and go and speak with your journalist friends.'

Nigel left the deputy's office and felt smug. He hadn't told him that he'd blackmailed both Rania and Othman. By the time that scam became public, both of them would be in it up to their necks and his misdemeanour would've been forgotten. He got into his car and made his way to Fleet Street contacting an old journalist mate on the way.

⊨⊣ ⊢⊨

Nick Roper had worked for *The Sun* for many years and was proud to be part of the gutter press. He had few principles and even less morals. But he was a good journalist, fearless in every way and didn't mind 'rocking the boat'. He despised celebrities believing that if they wanted the attention, he was going to give it, 'warts and all.' At one time he became a celebrity himself when he hounded a famous diva so much that she arranged to 'take him out' using a well- known contractor from the underworld. Unfortunately for her, the whole thing backfired as the contractor hadn't reckoned on Nick being a black belt in karate. Not that this in itself made any difference as the plan was to silence him with a gun. However, what won the day was Nick's reactions when confronted with a hooded figure outside an East End London pub. Before he even lifted the pistol to take aim Nick had him on the floor and was belting him with his right hand until the publican managed to restrain him. The police were called in and Nick was hailed a hero. He subsequently starred in his own newspaper and the diva was never seen or heard of again.

So Nick Roper was a bit of a maverick, a geezer, even a wide boy, but he did get his nose into awkward situations and was one of the best reporters - for digging up dirt - in the newspaper world. They'd agreed to meet in the *Bank of England* pub as there were plenty of corners in which to pass on information in relative secrecy.

When Nigel arrived, Nick was propping up the bar with a pint of bitter in his hands. He recognised Nigel immediately:

'What do you want officer Francis?'

'Pint of London Pride. Thanks Nick.'

'Drinking on duty officer?'

'Special dispensation for a copper who always gets his man.'

'Didn't know you liked men Nige, maybe I should order a pint of Gay Pride?'

'Very funny, but you're right, it's not always the men that need catching.'

'Tell me about it, the women are the worst.'

'Funny you should say that Nick. It's because of a woman I'm here.'

'Go on.'

'Do you remember the killing of Sir Michael Wilkinson, Head of MI5?'

'Yeah, let's sit down over here out of the way.'

'Well the prime suspect, a Ms Rania Hakim, was let off but I've raked up some new evidence.'

'So what?'

'I want you to publish.'

'It'll have to be good and I'll want a back hander.'

'No problem. I've met Rania and naturally she denies everything. More importantly I've met an Inspector Othman who was involved in the Dr Rob Williams case. To cut a long story short, he handed her a photograph which was found pinned on Sir Michael's jacket and he knows that Rania was the murderer?'

'How?'

'Because she told him?'

'So what.'

'I've got all our conversations recorded. I know Othman of old, we were university buddies. A smart cookie although hounded by principles.'

'What like me?'

'No, not like you. You're the most unprincipled git I've ever met.'

'Thank you officer, I love you too'.

'Listen, after I spoke to Rania I spoke to Othman who told me everything because we go back a long way and wanted to get Rania off the hook. You know that Rania and Dr Rob Williams were very close so when he was killed she had a motive for bumping off Sir Michael because both she and Othman were convinced the government were behind the killing.'

'They were probably right, although doubt whether it will ever be proved. But why did Othman tell you everything?'

'Because he trusted me and he believed the killing of Sir Michael was justified – honour kill-ing and all that Middle Eastern stuff. I told him murder was murder and the justice system was dif-ferent over here'.

'More's the pity.'

'Maybe, but there's enough evidence to resurrect the case and the Deputy Chief is with the Home Secretary as we speak.'

'Highly unlikely, but I'll take your word for it.'

'Now, Othman and Rania are pretty close and he'll stick his neck out for her. Trouble is, I guess, underneath, I'm a man of principle and Rania needs to be convicted. She murdered the Head of MI5.'

'Firstly, you're not a man of principle. Knowing you, you probably blackmailed them for your silence. They didn't cough up so that's why you're here.'

'How dare you, I'm a law enforcer not a lowlife like you.'

'Secondly, this is all hearsay and undercover espionage crap. It could have been anybody on that tape.'

'Look you dick head, when I play back the tape to Rania she'll collapse under pressure and confess. I know it.'

'Maybe, but what do you want me to say in the press. I've got to be careful. Don't want the Home Office suing my editor. That'll be curtains for me.'

'Where's your courage man? This woman is a murderer. I've got Inspector Othman on tape confirming the fact; I've got his disclosure that he handed over the photograph and when we get the two of them together we'll get a confession.'

'Okay. Have you got a copy of the tape?'

'Yes.'

'Well then, give it to me and I'll think about it.'

'No deal. I've parked my car round the corner. We both go there and you listen to the recording in my presence and I get to keep the tape. You can then tell me whether you're going to help me or not.'

'All right. But what's in it for you?'

'The glory – I always get my man?'

'Bullshit – let's go.'

⊶ ⊷

The next day, the main front page heading in *The SUN* read:

LET'S FIND SIR MICHAEL WILKINSON'S KILLER...

New evidence has been found in the case of Sir Michael Wilkinson, Head of MI5, who was brutally murdered on 29th May 2003 by an un-identified figure wearing a burkha. In a special announcement to the press yesterday Inspector Francis of the Metropolitan Police claims that he has established sufficient evidence through tape recordings to resurrect the case which was dropped last year following a statement from the Crown Prosecution Service. He states 'We have further evidence regarding the photograph of Sir Michael which was pinned to his jacket following his murder. This indicates that his killer owned this photograph - having received it, we suspect, from a member of the Cairo Police Force. Additional information involves a confession to this police officer that the prime suspect was guilty of this crime. An application to the Home Office will be made today for the resurrection of the case against this suspect. I think the whole country would agree that justice must be seen to be done and, at the moment, there is a murderer on the loose. So let's find the Head of MI5's killer and put this matter to rest once and for all.' Investigations continue.

Othman finished reading the headline and phoned Rania:

'Hi Rania, have you read the headlines?'

'Yes, but it's only in *The SUN.*'

'That's true but it's bound to get a mention on the television and radio, so brace yourself. Good thing is, no names have been mentioned which, I suppose, they can't do without the authority of the Home Office. Anyway, nothing changes. Sit tight and don't do a thing. If the Home Office gives permission then we have to get our stories straight.'

'What do you suggest?'

'Well, you can say that you were given the photograph by me but you lost it when you travelled to the UK. You can continue denying the murder and get your alibis to stand firm by their stories. As there were no witnesses I don't see how they can make a conviction.'

'What about my confession to you and your disclosure to your so called friend?'

'I'm thinking on that one. I can't lie. You did confess to the murder and I did disclose the same to Francis. In any case, don't worry too much because I don't know how strong that evidence will be in an English court – they might regard it as hearsay and declare it inadmissible. I don't know, we'll just have to wait and see. I suppose we could just deny everything. I could say that I've been impersonated and the voice on the tape is not mine. On the other hand, I can't lie. Sorry Rania, I'm rambling - going round in circles.'

Rania's mood changed and she said in a stern voice without a hint of compromise:

'You may be rambling but you're clear on the fact that you can't lie. You can't lie and yet you expect me to lie? This will get messy for both of us Othman, I'm warning you.'

'I know, but please just wait. Let's see what the Home Office has to say. If they give clearance we can meet up and agree our plan of action.

Inspector Francis can't do anything at the moment. If he approaches you, say nothing. I'll do the same. Meanwhile, I don't think we should meet up. You don't know what Nigel will be up to. If one of his cronies sees us together they'll use that to claim that we colluded and concocted our stories. Let's keep apart for the time being. Just act normally.'

'Okay Othman, that's going to be difficult. It feels like a great weight is hovering over my head, but I'll try my best.'

'Good, speak to you soon.'

Othman hung up, shaved, showered and got dressed. He was going to visit Magda today who had by now received a number of sessions of chemotherapy. It was one of those gloomy days in which everything seemed wrong. The train was too crowded, the ticket barriers weren't working, the hospital staff looked anxious and Othman was suffering from a headache. Things could only get better. But they didn't. As he was ascending the hospital stairs Mohammed came down the other way, clearly distressed.

'What's the matter Mo?'

'It's Magda, she's having terrible side effects.'

'Come here and sit down. That's only to be expected Mo. It shows that something's happening at least.'

'I know, but she's in so much discomfort. I can't bear to see her like this.'

'I know, I know. Let's see her and find out what we can do.'

They both went to the treatment room and saw Magda slouched in her chair. She had finished her session and looked as though she'd been hit by a devastating virus. Her hair was thinning and Othman could see parts of her scalp where the follicles had been completely destroyed. Her eyes were red and seemed motionless as she stared into nothingness through dark circles which had formed beneath her sockets. She looked pale and weak as she grabbed the arm rests tightly trying to regain some composure. She looked on the verge of collapsing and Mohammed quickly held her shoulders in an attempt to prevent her falling over. She had been sick which was evidenced by the bowl by her feet which had not been cleared away by the nurse. She tried to speak but she didn't have the strength. The two of them made a sorrowful pair with Mohammed sitting on the arm rest trying to comfort her and Magda bent over as she tried to ward off the nausea which came in waves. At times she would straighten up and stare at the wall as if she could see something beyond the tangible world. At other times she would simply slouch in her chair in what appeared to be an act of surrender.

'Now now Mrs Ishmail, what's the matter?' asked the nurse.

Magda looked up, shook her head and slumped back into her chair.

'I think she's hallucinating' Othman said.

'Probably, these drugs are very strong.'

'Drugs? I thought she was on one drug – Taxotere?'

'She was, but Mr Nathan has had to make a change.'

'Why?' asked Othman.

'You'll have to speak to him. We just do what we're told. She's on a combination of drugs now which have greater side effects.'

'What are they called?'

'It's known as TAC and combines a number of different drugs. We've also been instructed to increase the dosage. That's why Mrs Ishmail is feeling so awful at the moment. It'll soon pass and she'll be ready to go home in a few hours.'

'We weren't warned that she would have to change her drugs' said Mohammed.

'You'll have to speak to Mr Nathan about that.'

'I guess these drugs are more expensive?' asked Othman.

'You bet. They are much stronger so we should get better results. Mrs Ishmail's tumour is quite unusual so we want to give her the best treatment possible.'

'I see. We were told it was advanced and aggressive?' asked Mohammed.

'That's my understanding Mr Ishmail, but you'd better speak to Mr. Nathan about that. We certainly only administer TAC in high dosage for the more advanced cancers.'

After a couple of hours Magda felt stronger so the three of them left the Hospital and made their way to their hotel. Both Mohammed and Othman had to support Magda as she was clearly wobbly on her feet. The Ishmails would soon be transferring to rented property behind Euston Station which had been organised by Othman. Both Mohammed and Magda were looking forward to such a move as they felt they would have more independence living in their own apartment rather than residing in a large hotel where rules on fire procedures and the like had to be followed.

Othman was a bit confused about the change in drugs. Firstly, no one had notified them and secondly he recalled in his first conversation with Mohammed that Magda had been diagnosed with early stage cancer. This diagnosis may, of course, have been wrong, but he felt that he should do a little more research into this terrible disease. He wanted to be reassured, especially as he had financed part of the costs, that Magda was getting the right (as well as the best) treatment for the condition she had. He would do his research that afternoon and then arrange a meeting with Mr Nathan.

CHAPTER TWELVE

Richard Scott, Deputy Chief Constable of the Metropolitan Police phoned Nigel Francis and told him that, following the article in *The SUN* and a BBC broadcast on the six o'clock news, the Home Secretary had summoned both of them to his office. However, they were not to meet at Westminster but at the MI5 Headquarters on Millbank.

'I'll meet you in reception at two o'clock this afternoon Nigel.'

'But what about the chief, Richard, shouldn't you tell him?'

'Between you and me Nigel, his days are numbered. He's failed to meet crime targets and the ministers are out to get him. Keep that to yourself old boy. Looks like I could be next in line, fingers crossed.'

Nigel felt a pang of despair. All they'd be doing would be replacing one bureaucrat with another. These guys at the top, including all the politicians, didn't have a clue what was going on in the streets. All they cared about were their own careers. He paused and concluded that he was just as bad, the difference being that he was 'born and bred' in the gutters and knew exactly what was going on.

They both met as planned and were summoned to a room in the basement. On entering the room Nigel was shocked by the shabbiness of the decor. The walls needed repainting, there were no carpets, just lino, and the office furniture was something out of the thirties. There were metal stacking shelves hiding one wall accommodating files which looked like they hadn't been handled for a long time. The room resembled something between a store room and an old fashioned GP's dingy waiting room. The only thing missing was cigarette smoke and screaming kids. Nigel was expecting a plush conference room with state of the art communication systems, red carpet, pictures on the wall, a distinguished clock resting on a Queen Anne sideboard and bottles of Perrier water together with glasses on a silver plated tray. This was the very opposite – a dump with no windows.

However, there was a table and a number of chairs scattered across the room and the two of them were requested to take position on the opposite side of the table. They drew up their chairs and gazed with interest at the VIPs opposite.

Sitting in the middle was the Prime Minister (PM). Next to him on his right was the Home Secretary (HS) and on the other side was the new Head of MI5, Joshua Wilson-Smith who looked uncannily like a black version of Sir Michael Wilkinson. Next to Joshua was a man who introduced himself as Thomas DeVelt, MI5 Senior Operative.

The HS opened proceedings:

'I think we all know everybody here, or, at least, we'll all get to know each other by the end of this session. Needless to say what's said between these four walls is strictly confidential, any breach of which will be treated as an act of treason and a visit to the Tower.' There was a silence. 'Oh for god sake, lighten up, I'm only joking but I'm serious about confidentiality. Does everybody understand?' They all nodded. 'Now Richard, you tipped me off the other day about new evidence in the Sir Michael Wilkinson case. I told you to sit on it and yet *The SUN* broadcast it all over the country and the BBC talked about it last night. What an earth is going on?'

'Well sir, the killer has not been found and I have a duty to find them. It's as simple as that. Nigel here

has found new evidence which is sufficient to resurrect the case in my opinion. You see Nigel knows
the Cairo policeman who took charge of the Dr Rob
Williams case. They go back a long way. Inspector
Othman, the name of the policeman is over here on
personal business and the two of them met up.'

'Is this true Inspector Francis?'

'Yes sir.'

'Carry on Richard – and make it good.'

'Well in their conversation Othman admitted
handing over Sir Michael's photo to Rania Hakim,
the prime suspect, and told Nigel that Rania had
confessed to him that she did in fact murder Sir
Michael.'

'Why did he tell the Inspector all this?'

'Because Nigel had already spoken to Rania who
was, shall we say, a bit defensive about the whole matter. She must've spoken to Othman who she knows
very well, and he, in a bid to protect her disclosed everything to Nigel, hoping he would forget the whole
thing – them being university buddies and all that.'

'Sorry, you've lost me' said the PM 'Firstly why
were you Inspector Francis speaking to Rania
Hakim when you knew the case against her had
been dropped?'

'Call it a cop's intuition sir. I didn't believe the police had done a great job in charging her and there
were definite questions marks over this photograph.'

'So what? You had no business interviewing her.'

'I know sir and I was out of order. But the bigger picture is that we have new evidence in this case and the public want justice.'

'You sound a bit naive Inspector. What I don't understand is that after this interview you met with Inspector Othman who revealed all in the hope you would keep quiet. Why didn't you keep quiet – loyalty to a friend and all that good will stuff?'

'Because I'm a cop sir. My job is to catch the villains.'

'Oh really Inspector, thanks for the enlighten-ment - I often wondered why we employ coppers. Now I know'.

'Sorry sir.'

'So you had the story. Why did you need to go to the press?'

'Two reasons sir. Firstly, to put pressure on the establishment to resurrect the case against Rania Hakim and, secondly, to threaten – that is, if they didn't own up, to publicise their story in the press.'

'I'm still not following you. You had the story so why go to the press?'

'As I said sir, I was trying to frighten them. They didn't play ball so I went to the press.'

'So you threatened them?' Was money involved Inspector – you'd better tell me everything.'

'Yes sir, I told them that if they made a donation I wouldn't go to the press.'

'And who would this donation be made to?'

'Me sir'

'So you blackmailed them?'

'All in the line of duty sir – end justifies the means as Machiavelli would say. I would have passed the donation to the Police Federation or to the local cat charity ... of course'

'Would you now Inspector'. There was a pause. 'The fact is Machiavelli no longer operates and you've discredited the police force. You know this is a sackable offence Mr Francis?'

'Service sir, not force.' said the HS.

'Yes, yes I know that, for goodness sake man, don't get pedantic on me now. But what's happened here is that Inspector Francis has blackmailed both Rania Hakim and Inspector Othman. Let me guess, I bet Othman refused to be blackmailed, refused to hand over the money and so our Inspector friend here gave the press the story. Now it's in the public arena you're hoping we'll resurrect the case.'

'In a nutshell Richard is this the case?' asked the HS.

'Yes sir, I'm afraid it is.'

'You two are not looking good from where I stand.' said the PM. 'In fact Inspector Francis you have committed a criminal offence.'

'I know that sir, and I was wrong. I see that now. But we have good evidence as a basis for resurrecting the case.'

'What evidence?'

Nigel played them the tapes.

'You know this may not be admissible?'

'We know that sir' said Nigel 'But I strongly believe once Rania Hakim hears these tapes, she'll confess to the murder.'

'May be, may be not' said the HS. 'What is clear to me Inspector is that you have not followed proper protocols and although you may be on to something, it's not in this country's interest to resurrect this case. It would open up old wounds and prompt further investigations into the Rob Williams affair. The government doesn't want this – I'm sure you'll understand. Whilst it had no involvement in the unfortunate and callous murder of Dr Rob Williams it doesn't want the public to be reminded of the event. A resurrection of the Sir Michael case would bound to lead to further questions being asked, umpteen investigations and further use of resources which we haven't got. The longer the case goes on the more likely the government would be implicated. Let sleeping dogs lie Mr Francis. We thank you for your enthusiasm and for bringing this matter to our attention. It will not go unnoticed, especially when the promotions board meet.'

'I agree' said the PM 'Let us handle matters from this point on. On no account go back to the press. If they hound you simply say that investigations will continue and that there is no more to report. Say nothing more. I will be watching closely. If anything untoward appears on the television or in the newspapers, I will hold you both accountable. Don't let it happen. I am prepared to forgive your sins, but don't let this happen again. Remember, no more blackmail, no more press. The case is finished as far as you're concerned. Do I have your understanding and acceptance gentlemen?'

'Yes sir' they both chimed.

'Good. Now good afternoon gentlemen.'

Richard and Nigel left the MI5 Headquarters with mixed feelings. On one hand they knew they had enough to get the case resurrected, on the other, they liked the idea of promotion if they kept quiet. They both agreed that they were as bad as each other in their quest for self- advancement.

Meanwhile, back in the basement the HS suggested that there was probably sufficient evidence to resurrect the case but there existed sound political reasons for not doing so. But then there was the matter of the judicial system and, clearly, Rania Hakim had murdered Sir Michael and, clearly, Inspector Othman had been an accessory. It wouldn't take the police service, CPS and the criminal law courts long to come to these conclusions and, as all these institutions came under the jurisdiction of the Home Office, justice could be fast tracked under this authority alone and the appropriate punishment administered. The PM confirmed that this was a Home Office issue and would leave it to the Secretary to sort out. He left the building and was chauffeured back to Number 10.

The Secretary turned to the Head of MI5 and said:

'What do you think Josh?'

'Well sir, we have a murderer on the loose and we know who she is, where she works and who has helped her. Sir Michael was a personal friend of mine and you simply cannot have this killer walking around the streets of London.'

'What do you suggest?'

'Both Rania Hakim and Inspector Othman know too much. We need to arrange for their silence.'

'How, send them back to Cairo and brand them as terrorists?'

'Perhaps, but they can still talk whether they're in Cairo or London.'

'Your point?'

'I believe, in the interests of national security, a more longer term solution should be found.'

'Well, I'll leave that to MI5 to sort out. Keep me and the PM out of any, shall we say, underhand activity. Let's just say that I agree with you – this matter has to be 'nipped in the bud'.

'Leave it with me sir.'

The Home Secretary got up from his chair and made for the exit. When he reached the door he turned round and said:

'Whatever you do Josh, keep the government out of it.'

'Good day sir. As I've said, leave it with me.'

When the Secretary had gone Joshua turned to Thomas Develt:

'Right Tom, you know what you've got to do?'

'Yes sir.'

'Good. Usual protocols apply – no witnesses, no evidence and no suspects.'

'Timing sir?'

'Immediate. Oh, and another thing our intelligence tells us that Othman is over here with friends. Something about helping a woman with breast cancer at UCH. Rather than approach the suspects direct I suggest you track their whereabouts via the hospital. The more complex and diverse you can make your investigations, the easier it will be to fulfil your assignment without blemish – there'll be so many fingers pointing in so many directions that your identity will be hard to pinpoint. Anyway, make it that way.'

'It's even better than that sir. I've already done my research. I found out that her oncologist is Mr James Nathan –an old university buddy of mine.'

'Be careful – make sure he's on our side.'

'No problem sir we go back a long way. We played polo together at university.'

'Wonderful. Keep me posted and good luck.'

'Don't need luck sir, I'll keep in contact.'

CHAPTER THIRTEEN

Rania busied herself as best she could at work trying not to think of the predicament she found herself. She put on a brave face although none of the museum staff knew about her background so there was nothing to worry about from this perspective. Of course her flat mates knew about her circumstances as they had acted as alibis in support of her case. They had become excellent friends and promised to stand by their statements even though, in doing so, they would perjure themselves. Thankfully they were both Muslims and believed Rania's story that the government, in the form of Sir Michael Wilkinson, were behind Dr Rob's killing. They figured he'd got his just desserts and were prepared to stand up in court and say so. They would also corroborate Rania's story that she was with them at the time of the killing.

All of this, however, did not prevent Rania from feeling extremely anxious. Say if the case were resurrected? This would mean more cross examination and more lies– not to mention the pressure Othman would be put under if he were accused of aiding and abetting. There was a side of her which said that she ought to own up – confess her sin and rely on the mitigating circumstances to reduce her punishment. On the other hand, would anybody care about her claim that the government were behind Rob's killing? Would the public believe her? Even if they did, a murder had been committed and the people would want justice.

She knew in her heart she had done the right thing as she was convinced Sir Michael had sanctioned Rob's killing and, from this point of view, the assassination had been justified. She must stick to her guns and, if she is cross examined, keep to the story she'd agreed with Othman.

While pondering on these thoughts she didn't notice Professor Angus Lear enter the office:

'You look down my Iraqi princess, tell me all.'

'I'm fine,' she said 'just one of those days.'

'One of those days...what a strange expression. Every day is *one of those days* my dear. We just have to pick ourselves up and think about the good things in life. I mean, look at me – handsome, young, intelligent and witty. What more could I ask? And yet you reject my advances; you punish me so severely with your apathy and contempt. So you see, I suffer *one of those days* every day when I see you; and yet, do you see me cry? Do you see me down? Do you see me wretch at the very thought of your persistent rejection? No, I soldier on, I get on with life, I smile, I laugh, I tell jokes, I make people happy. I'm like the circus clown who laughs on the outside but is broken within. Broken because my love for you is not reciprocated. Broken because I know you need me but refuse to express these needs in a way which would free you from your torment. I am a broken man Rania, and it's all your fault.'

Rania spirits lifted with this buffoonery.

'Professor, the only thing you've said that has any credence is that you view yourself as a clown. You are a clown and I'll put in a grievance if you don't stop your clowning. Funny you are not; young you are not; desirous of me you are not. All in all professor, when it comes to wooing, you're an idiot.'

'No, no, no. I don't believe you. Don't shatter my dreams, my life, my very being. I will not take this rejection'.

The professor changed his mood and became more serious:

'Now, tell me what's wrong. It's obvious to me and everybody else in this office that you are upset. Let's go into the quiet area. I might be able to help you.'

They took their coffees and went to the quiet room. Rania sat on the sofa and began to cry. It was as if everything had been building up inside and, now that her sad demeanour had been noticed, her emotions rocketed to the surface.

'I can't tell you Angus. I wish I could, but I just... I just can't.'

'Whatever it is it can't be that bad, unless of course you've killed someone.' Angus joked.

'No, it's nothing like that' she lied. 'Before I came here I worked at the Cairo Museum.'

'We all knew that Rania.'

'Yes, I know. But before that I met a man in Iraq. I fell in love with him. He was a married man and went back to England. I went to Cairo. I got badly harassed and this good man came back to protect me. He got killed for his efforts.'

'Oh no Rania. That's terrible, When did this happen?'

'Over a year ago.'

'And you haven't come to terms with it?'

'That's right.'

'Well my dear, time is a great healer and although you'll never forget him, things will get better. I'm sure of it.'

'I know but I did an awful thing which cannot be forgiven.'

'What's that?'

'I took revenge on his killer.'

'That's not so awful if you were ridding the world of a killer – I'm assuming your revenge took the form of murder?'

'Yes.'

'Okay, that was wrong, of course, but you had a good motive, there was justification. I know a little bit about the Middle East. If you hadn't executed him the authorities would have done. You've got to look at it like that Rania. From where you come from it's an eye for an eye, tooth for a tooth philosophy which I sometimes think should be the practice over here. Did the Egyptian authorities know that you had committed this crime?'

'I don't think so'.

'So is this why you came over here -   to escape prosecution?'

'There were other reasons.'

'Of course, and I won't pry into these. Look Rania, you're a good person and you're part of the team here. What's done is done and you have to find a way of moving on. I promise you, your secret is safe with me. And another thing, if you need any help, please let me know. Despite all my buffoonery I'm a principled person and believe what you've told me.

Had the murder been committed in this country, then that would've been a different matter. Our laws are not the same, more's the pity, and despite your justification, you would've been convicted for murder. Thank god the killing took place in Egypt.'

'Yes, thank God'she lied again.

'Right we'll keep this between ourselves and I won't mention it again. Has this little chat helped?'

'It has Angus, thank you so much. I think I've said too much, but I had to. It's been building up inside me for so long. I feel a sense of relief now that I've confided in you. Please keep our conversation confidential. I don't want the whole world to know about my confession.'

'Trust me Rania. As I have said, your secret is safe with me. Let's get back to the office. And don't forget, call me if you need me.'

'Thanks Angus.'

That night Rania phoned Othman and told him that she'd confided in Angus. He asked why she had done that and she replied she had no one else to talk to and was becoming paranoid. She explained she hadn't told him the true story and felt confident that Angus wasn't the sort of man to breach a confidence.

'I told him that I killed Rob's murderer in Egypt and made no mention of the political side of things. I told him that I was being harassed and that Rob came to help me and lost his life as a consequence.'

'Did you mention any names?'

'Certainly not. All Angus knows is that I killed someone in Egypt in revenge for the death of my lover.'

'You shouldn't have said anything to anybody. We can't trust Angus even though he appears like a nice bloke. Word gets around. A few drinks at the office party and promises get broken. You shouldn't have done that Rania.'

'I had no choice. I had to tell someone. I'm going out of my mind with worry. I think I'm on the verge of a breakdown.'

'I get that. I do sympathise but we must keep to our plan – say and do nothing, keep your head down and wait. Hopefully there'll be no more press releases and the matter will die away. I'm sure the Home Office won't want to resurrect the whole case again so just stay calm. If you need to talk to anybody, talk to me.'

'Okay Othman, I'll try to keep calm but I'm coming to the end of my tether. I feel like getting the next plane out.'

'I know, I know, but that would raise even more suspicion so just sit tight. Don't forget, Nigel will be monitoring your every movement so don't think you can get out of the country unnoticed.'

'I know that but it's so hard.'

'Sure, speak to you later.'

Rania packed her bags. She had thoughts of making a run for it.

CHAPTER FOURTEEN

The next day Othman phoned Nathan's secretary and organised an appointment for that afternoon. All three of them took the tube, the Ishmails having got used to the frantic hustle and bustle of underground life, and waited for the next train to Warren Street. Their journey was uneventful with neither Mohammed nor Magda wishing to make polite conversation. They sat in the carriage holding hands looking as though they were embarking on their final journey; not saying a word but peering intently at their reflections in the black windows opposite. They were a picture of misery! Both dreaded confronting Mr Nathan and were glad that Othman was there to support them. They had been brought up not to question authority and the thought of questioning Nathan about his treatment package filled them with dread.

Othman, on the other hand, was different. He'd spent a large part of his life in the UK and, indeed, the USA, and he had no qualms about questioning things he didn't understand. He'd spent some time in the morning researching breast cancer and the types of treatment available both within the NHS and private sector. He discovered that if cancer were caught early enough, it could be completely cured. He also discovered that there were many drugs used in chemotherapy and that the treatment and the use of these drugs varied depending on the needs of the patient. The Ishmails had been told that Magda's cancer was rare, more advanced than originally thought, and aggressive. On the other hand, Mohammed had told him that her cancer was in the early stages and that the only reason it couldn't be treated immediately was that there was such a long waiting list in Cairo. Mr Gustav then announced that this was not the case and that her best chance of a cure was to go to the UK for more expensive treatment. On researching the drugs being administered to Magda, he found that the latest medication was probably right if her cancer were of the type that had been explained to them. This being the case he was uncertain why she was given a milder drug to begin with. The other mystery was that it had never been explained to them why she could not be operated on before her chemotherapy treatment. He had read that in many cases, the tumour was removed surgically to begin with, and then the body was treated with chemotherapy and radiotherapy. Mr Nathan had gone straight into chemotherapy, with a milder drug more associated with early stage cancer, rather than operate. He was sure that Nathan would have answers to all these questions but felt determined to put his concerns to him. He went into a reverie...He thought - we all believe what our doctors tell us, but suppose they're not telling us the truth? Why would they not tell us the truth? Because they don't like giving us bad news? Because they have something to hide? Or because there's money to be made? Everything comes down to money, even the financial opportunities presented in the use of medicine. Take someone with a headache going to a private practice. What's stopping a consultant charging for a CAT scan when an aspirin might solve the problem? The medical profession is shrouded in mystery. If a doctor recommends a procedure we accept it without question. Doctor knows best. But say if this procedure is not really necessary? The patient has no ability to question its application and simply accepts the situation and pays the bills. Could this be the same for cancer treatment? Does Magda really need the course of drugs she's been given? Othman was going to find out.

They arrived for their appointment on time and Mr Nathan ushered them into his office.

'Do you want a drink? The machine here is not very good but I can guarantee something wet and hot', he joked.

'No thank you said Othman.'

'How about yourselves?'

'No thanks' the Ishmails replied in unison.

'Right, how can I help, the treatment seems to be going well although I understand Mrs Ishamil has had a rather bad reaction to the latest drugs?'

'That's an understatement' said Mohammed. 'She's on the verge of giving up on her treatment.'

'Oh come come Mr Ishmail, I appreciate the effects are horrible, but it will only last for a short period of time. You must try to stick with it Mrs Ishmail.'

'Easier said than done doctor' said Magda.

'Mr not doctor Mrs Ishmail, address me as Mr if you don't mind.'

'Sorry doctor, I mean Mr Nathan, I didn't know.'

'Of course of course, now is there anything else?'

'Yes there is', piped up Othman. 'Magda was originally diagnosed as having early stage breast cancer. How come this has changed?'

'Early diagnosis is not always accurate Mr Othman. Sometimes the results are misleading and it's only when we do further tests that the true nature of the disease emerges. Besides, even if it were an early stage cancer, it certainly isn't now as, as you know, cancers can grow at varying pace. Even if it was early stage, the pace of growth in Mrs Ishmail's case has been extraordinary.'

'Okay but why was she not operated on straight away. I understand normal practice is to cut out the tumour, check the lymph glands and follow this up with chemo and radiotherapy.'

'Quite right in normal circumstances. However, our x rays show that the tumour is inoperable at this stage and that the disease has spread to the lymph glands. We must reduce the size of the tumour as well as treat other parts of the body, where the cancer may have spread, using the strongest of drugs, before performing an operation. I am optimistic that the treatment will work and that we will be able to operate on Mrs Ishmail very soon. Please be reassured.'

'Why then was she given a mild drug to begin with? Why was she not given the more toxic drug straight away?'

'It's a question of weaning Mr Othman. We wanted Mrs Ishmail's body to get used to cancer fighting drugs and it was my opinion that the best way to start, in her case, was to start with a milder drug.'

'Okay but we would like to see all the test results including x rays, scans, bloods and urine samples as soon as possible Mr Nathan.'

'Naturally, I can arrange this, but it will take some time. I will have to sit with you of course to interpret the results. Most of it will be jargon to you.'

'Are all her results kept here?'

'Yes, I can get them out now if you wish. Perhaps you would like to take a seat in reception while I collect the files together.'

The three of them waited for hours in the reception area while Mr Nathan requested his assistant to collect the pertinent files. Meanwhile he wafted round the hospital, checking on his other patients, talking to his nurses, joking with the reception staff and generally passing the time of day with his colleagues. Othman didn't trust him although couldn't rationalise his mistrust. He knew that any question he gave would be answered in full – with only half of it being understood. He pondered again... he thought - we only truly know what's wrong with us when the organ or a bit of tissue is cut out, displayed and analysed – all these tests are not 100% accurate. They could be wrong.

Nathan's secretary ushered them back into his room and sat them opposite an x ray slide.

'Right, this shows the size of the tumour. Look, it has spread beyond the nipple area and has covered a large part of the breast.' Nathan pointed to the slide as he spoke. 'This x ray shows the lymph glands and, as you can see, this area has been affected.'

Magda couldn't cope with such information and became visibly distressed:

'I've had enough' Magda cried. 'I don't want to see any more. I want to go home. As far as I'm concerned Mr Nathan is doing all he can and I've just got to get on with it. I find this whole thing distressing. I don't want to know anymore. Can we go home Mohammed?'

'Of course my dear and I'm sorry we've put you through this. Thank you Mr Nathan, you've showed us enough. We'll let you get on with the treatment. After all, you know best.'

'That's fine Mr Ishmail. Anytime you and your wife want to come back, be my guests. We're here to support you at all times.'

They left Nathan's room and made their way slowly down the stairs. Othman bid them farewell and went back to the reception area. He pondered...how do we know they were Magda's x rays? We didn't question whether these related to her – we just assumed they did. Othman decided to stay. He was going to figure out some way of breaking into Nathan's office. Desperate times demanded desperate measures.

⊨⊣ ⊢⊨

He sat in the main reception area and observed the activities. There were a number of security guards milling around the main exit and, like bees returning to the hive, they occasionally darted across the entrance hall towards their office which was situated near the men's toilets. Othman made his way to this office and peered in. There were monitors, screens and switchboards and it didn't take Othman long to realise that all departments and offices were under surveillance. This together with the number of security guards would make any attempt to break into Nathan's room risky to say the least. The last thing he wanted was to be caught in the act. In any case, specialists might not keep medical records in their offices and so even if he managed to break in unnoticed, his venture may prove to be futile.

He asked the main receptionist whether there was a separate medical records department and was told that all records were stored in the basement under the control of the Medical Records Manager – a Miss Humpkins. He was also told that the only people who could view their files were the patients or, if they had been declared mentally unfit, a representative officially nominated through the appropriate channels.

Othman decided that Magda would have to make a personal request. He quickly exited the hospital and made his way to the Ishmail's residence.

The following morning Othman with a very worried looking Magda found themselves facing a rosy cheeked and rather plumpish lady who introduced herself as Miss Humpkins.

'Have you got proof of identity Mrs Ishmail?' She asked.

Magda presented her passport and her outpatient card. Miss Humpkins studied her screen and, after a few seconds, her face lit up.

'Ah yes. Here we are. Mrs Magda Ishmail. Right, let me check with the breast clinic. Please take a seat.'

'No' said Othman. 'You don't have to check with anyone. Mrs Ishmail has a right to see her records and no further authority is required. I've read up on medical ethics, so please just hand over all her files.'

'But our procedures say that we must check first.'

'Then your procedures are wrong. Look I don't won't to appear rude but it is important that Magda sees her files. After all, it's her body we're talking about and she has the right to find out what's been said about her.'

'Look Mr...'

'Othman.'

'Look Mr Othman, no one is saying that she cannot see her files but I have to check with the oncologist first.'

'Why?'

'It's procedure.'

'Never mind procedure Miss Humpkins. Why? The oncologist must know what's in the file so why do you need to check? Unless, of course, the hospital is trying to hide something?'

'Of course not Mr. Othman.'

'Good, then there should be no reason why Magda can't see her files immediately.'

'I suppose not, but it's not normal procedure.'

'Well, put it this way, if you don't disclose the files immediately I'll let the BMA know that not only are you being uncooperative, but you're following un-ethical procedures - and that won't look good for the hospital or yourself. Now please, show Magda where the files are kept and give her a quiet moment to look through them.'

'Very well' said Miss Humpkins who was now looking flustered and just wanted the two of them to do what they had come to do and leave.

She led them out to the records which were stored in massive metal vaults, turned a rather large handle and beckoned them down a gangway where thousands of files were shelved. She stopped at the shelf marked 'HIJ' and, after a minute or so, found Magda's file. Othman peered over her shoulder to make sure there was only one Magda Ishmail. Fortunately there was and so he urged Magda to take the file immediately. Once it was in her hands the mission was almost complete.

'Where can I read these?' Magda asked.

They stepped out of the gangway and were directed towards a table.

'Please give Magda a couple of minutes Miss Humpkins. She promises not to steal anything.'

'Okay, but only a couple of minutes. I've already breached procedures and don't intend to break any more.'

Miss Humpkins just wanted them out of her department and in her hurry forgot that Othman was still there and, in her panic, forgot another hospital rule – that she should be present while the patient read through the files.

When she was gone Othman opened up the file and quickly found the following: a note confirming that Magda had early stage grade one cancer which, in all probability, had not spread to any other area beyond the immediate tumour site ; a note which confirmed an operation to remove the tumour at the first opportunity; a note from a Mr Gustav to Mr Nathan stating she would need more advanced treatment in the UK and that agreed protocols should apply; a recent specimen result which showed that her urine and stools were normal, and a breakdown of costs showing the difference between standard and advanced treatments. Othman couldn't interpret the x rays but believed he had enough evidence to create a stir. He quickly photographed each document and slid his camera in his pocket. As he did so Miss Humpkins entered the room and asked Othman to leave as he should not have accompanied Magda in the first place.

'Of course Miss Humpkins. I'm so sorry. I'll go immediately. Thank you very much for your cooperation. I'll leave Magda to it. Goodbye.' Othman left the room and waited outside the department.

'Now, Mrs Ishmail, please go ahead and read through the files.'

'Thank you' said Magda as she flipped over the papers with her eyes tightly shut.

After about five minutes Magda met Othman in the corridor and asked him what he'd photographed. He explained that in all probability she had early stage cancer and yet for some reason the doctors had changed this diagnosis to advanced stage without, it seemed, any supporting evidence. He told her that he might've got this wrong, but felt suspicious about the whole thing. He tried to explain that he thought this may be part of a scam whereby doctors charge for expensive drugs and procedures even though cheaper ones would be just as effective. Magda was mystified and couldn't believe that respectable doctors would mislead their patients in such a way. She was angry and upset but most of all confused.

'We now have to confront Mr Nathan with this information Magda and get you properly treated.'

'But I don't want to question him Othman.'

'You don't have to. Let's forget about protocols for one minute. I think there's some sort of medical scam going on and we have no time for niceties. I'll ask the questions, don't worry.'

They made their way to Nathan's office. Fortunately his door was ajar and he sat there alone. Othman burst into his office with Magda trailing behind him.

'What's going on?' Nathan asked.

'Sit down Mr Nathan and listen to me.'

'I will not. Nurse, call security!'

'Call them if you like but look at these photos first. You may not want anybody else to know about your little scam with Mr Gustav.'

'Nurse, it's all right. Please close the door and don't call security. I can sort out this little misunderstanding.'

Othman and Magda sat down opposite Nathan and showed him the photographs.

'So what' said Nathan. 'This doesn't mean anything. As I've said before, cancers can quickly change from early stage to advanced. This is the case here I assure you.'

'I don't believe you' said Othman. 'It doesn't stack up. Within a very short timescale a grade one cancer has changed to advanced: you advised us that there was blood in Magda's urine and stools when there wasn't; you get a note from your friend Gustav saying advanced treatment is needed when it wasn't, and a note reveals the difference in costs. It's obvious that you're going to charge at the higher rate, treat her at the lower rate and pocket the difference.'

'But she's on the most expensive drug at the moment. What profit is to be made out of that?'

'Well first of all, I doubt whether she needs such advanced treatment. I've read up on grade one breast cancer and the first thing to do is to cut the tumour out – not apply advanced highly toxic chemotherapy. The second thing is this. You knew that Magda would have a bad reaction to the more toxic drug but you wanted the whole thing to look credible. You told us she had advanced cancer so the more toxic drug would look like the next logical step. As you said, you weaned her on the first drug so that she would be less vulnerable to the second. However, at this early stage you'd not be making a profit so, following reports from Magda that she couldn't stomach the second dose of drugs, you were going to put her on the cheaper one but charge for the more expensive and from that point, make some money.'

'But that's just conjecture. You have no proof of that.'

'Either that, or you were just going to keep her on the expensive drugs and charge at the higher rate for your own personal gain – after all, it's the hospital that probably pays for the drugs, not you, so it doesn't matter either way. The fact of the matter is that we don't trust you and intend taking it up with the powers that be.'

'Look Inspector Othman, I am a prominent physician. Do you think I would get involved with any under- hand activity concerning my profession? You are not qualified to make the statements you're making and have no real medical evidence to prove your case.'

'May be not, but all this doesn't look good for you. There's enough here to instigate an inquiry. You can't play around with people's lives. You're not God and unless you can provide us with some damn good explanations I'm going to the press.'

'But you can't do that. You'll look a fool. You're not part of the medical fraternity and don't know what you're saying. I will stand by the diagnosis and say to the world that Mrs Ishmail is receiving the best possible treatment for her cancer. You as a layman have no proof that I'm not giving her such treatment.'

'Look Mr Nathan, as I've said, I reckon I have enough here to prompt a full blown enquiry. I know I'm not part of the medical fraternity but that won't stop me from pursuing the matter, you better believe it. Magda will now want a second opinion and I can assure you, that opinion will be sought elsewhere. Come on Magda, let's go.'

Mr. Nathan got out of his chair and looked out the window. He poured himself a glass of water and sat on his desk. He was angry and a little worried. He picked up his phone:

'Is that you Miss Humpkins, I need to see you urgently. Come up straightaway and bring the Ishmail file with you.'

CHAPTER FIFTEEN

Thomas DeVelt was the son of a Dutch merchant who had made his fortune exporting prints of 'Old Master' paintings. His mother was English and had met his father in a hippie commune just outside Amsterdam. They were both intelligent and, after their drug and psychedelic experiences, became very ambitious and turned their backs on the 'free love' society. They became successful landowners in Buckinghamshire, decided to have a child, and produced Thomas.

Thomas did well in his studies and became a keen sportsman. He got a first at Cambridge and joined the Civil Service. He was big, gruff and, like his parents, ambitious. Unlike his parents he developed a bully-ing manner which he found successful in getting what he wanted. He had always been a bully. At school he bullied the smaller kids and at university he bullied his colleagues on the rugby field. He was intelligent from an academic perspective but ignorant from a so-cial one. He progressed in life through bullying oth-ers less fortunate than him – ensuring that his rivals failed – whilst honouring his superiors to the extent that, provided he achieved personal gain, any sacri-fice, principled or otherwise, was worth it. He was a survivor, manipulator, bully and became, as time went by, a ruthless MI5 operative.

He lived in a one bed roomed flat on the Isle of Dogs which looked out on to the Thames. The de-cor was minimalist with white painted rooms, white kitchen units and white furniture. This vision of whiteness suited Thomas who had no time for clut-ter preferring a clinical approach to life. There was just one picture on the wall which was a reproduc-tion of Lowry's 'Matchstick Men' and had been pur-chased for the sole reason of hiding a mark which he couldn't be bothered to paint over. Apart from this, only a stainless steel clock, which hung in the lounge, gave any indication or insight into the per-sonal world of operative Develt.

He sat down on his white leather sofa, after a hard day's work, and pondered on the day's events. He had met with the Prime Minister, Home Secretary, Deputy Chief of the Metropolitan Police, Head of MI5 and some jumped up police inspector who wasn't worth bothering about. Since being promoted to senior operative he had waited patiently for an assignment which was commensurate with his new status. At last one had been given – a job for *Queen and Country* – the secret disposal of two foreign enemies of the state. He wasn't interested in the circumstances or the background events, although he knew what they were. He was only interested in the fact that his country had asked him to carry out an assignment in the interests of national security. This is all he cared about. He sat there content with his lot, drinking a rather large measure of whisky. The phone rang:

'Hi Tom, James.'

'Hi James, you won't believe this but I was about to phone you to organise our monthly game of squash,'

'How's the Secret Service?'

'Same as usual, can't say a word. What about the medical profession?'

'About the same, but I may have a bit of a problem.'

'Go on.'

'I better explain on the squash court out of everyone's way.'

'Does it have anything to do with Rania Hakim or Inspector Othman?'

'Never heard of Rania Hakim but, yes, I do have a problem with a Mr Othman. How on earth did you fathom this out? What's the connection?'

'Right, stop there. Might be able to help out. It's a funny old world because I was going to make contact with you about the same man.'

'Oh, really? Well, perhaps we can do some business – old university buddies and all that stuff.'

'Quite. Can you make 10.00 tomorrow?'

'Where?'

'At the club'

'I'll see you there'.

———

The club was situated off the Chelsea Embankment and on first glance looked like an old Edwardian manor house. It had a massive front door and the whole frontage was covered in ivy. Only the large windows had escaped this aggressive foliage, and this had only been achieved by constant trimming and cut back by a gardener whose only ambition in life was to annihilate ivy on a global basis – he hated the stuff! However, he was restrained by the owners who rather liked the idea of their club's facade being covered with the green stuff as, in their view, it gave a country gentry feel which complimented the prestigious image they were trying to promote. The club had just one squash court and one bar. The membership fee was just under £10,000 per year and attracted the very highest classes in English society. This included billionaires, royalty and ex pubic school boys. Women were not allowed and it was recognised that most members hadn't picked up a squash ball in their lives. The real purpose of the club was to facilitate 'business discussion' (which could include anything provided it meant personal gain and/ or protection) between high ranking officials which could be conducted in the many private areas available on the ground floor while having easy access to the bar. Having said this Tom and James were excellent squash players and used the facility quite often for this purpose as most other members had no interest in such an energetic sport.

Thomas arrived early and headed straight for the dressing rooms. He changed into his gear and started warming up on the court. There was no public gallery, no CCTV and very few people used the changing rooms. Accordingly the court was the ideal place for conducting confidential discussions, and Tom and James often held such conversations, continuing their talks in the shower, the changing rooms and, finally, the bar.

Today was no exception and after warming up Thomas asked James what he knew about Inspector Othman:

'Nothing much really, except that he is taking an over active interest in the treatment of one of my patients.'

'What do you mean?'

'Well, I'm treating a patient with cancer and charging her at the higher rate. He seems to think that she doesn't need such advanced treatment and is suggesting that I'm involved in some kind of scam.'

'But what does he know about cancer treatment?'

'Precisely.'

'I assume you're acting ethically James?'

'Of course. Okay, I may be airing on the side of caution and giving her drugs that may be viewed by some as going over the top, but that's all down to my opinion as to what the best course of treatment should be.'

'Are you personally making any money out of this? In other words could you be treating her with less expensive drugs and achieving the same result?'

'That's hard to say. The less expensive drugs may not achieve the same result. We don't know.'

'Are you telling me everything James. After all, why would Othman accuse you of being part of a scam?'

'You'll have to ask him. The thing is Tom, he's becoming a nuisance and he could cause trouble. Is there any way you can help me?'

'What do you mean?'

'Well, he's Egyptian or Sudanese, I think. He must be on a visitor visa or something. Can you not put pressure on him to bugger off back to the Middle East? There must be something you guys can do to make him illegal?'

'It doesn't work like that James. I have no powers at the Home Office so I can't help you there.'

'Well is there anything you can do?'

'You sound worried James. Maybe this guy does have something on you?'

'Oh, don't you start Tom. Look, okay, I may be making a little money out of this treatment, but a lot of doctors take advantage of the system – that's the way it is.'

'Let's cut to the chase. As it happens MI5 are not too keen on this individual for reasons I can't disclose. I might be able to help you in an unofficial capacity if you can do three things.'

'What are they?'

'Give me his contact number, the patient's name and reimburse my expenses.'

'And how much will that be?'

'It will depend on what I find out. Let's just say for now, it's likely to cost you in the region of £10,000.'

'That seems a lot of money?'

'Do you want me to help you or not?'

'Okay, but I want this guy out of the way.'

'Got you.'

After this brief but focussed discussion the two of them locked horns in a 'best out of three' contest. James was the more wily combatant while Thomas was the more aggressive. The first set was fairly even with both players getting into their stride, but the second and third sets were ferocious with long rallies, many grunts and occasional groans. The sweat was quickly pouring off them and the game turned into war. Neither of them were good losers and although they had mutual respect for each other, by the end of the last set the rivalry was so acute that their 'friendship', if that's the right word, turned into loathing which resulted in disbelief on the part of James who was eventually beaten by Thomas, although, he would say, he was robbed and the best man lost. However, by the time they'd showered, dressed and finished their second of two large whiskies, they'd forgotten the game and focussed on the club's objectives – personal gain and protection.

CHAPTER SIXTEEN

While Thomas was driving back to his flat he thought through his strategy. At the moment, neither Rania nor Othman knew whether the case against her was going to be resurrected. Othman would be just as troubled as Rania as he had been implicated. Accordingly, he wanted to see Othman immediately, firstly, because he (Othman) would have a lot more information on his mate's dubious medical practices; secondly, because his current vulnerability made it less likely that Othman would disclose the fact that Thomas had left MI5 operative Katerine O 'Reilly to die in the Rob Williams case and thirdly; it didn't really matter either way because he was going to kill Othman as soon as he could!

What he wanted at this stage was more information on Nathan so that he could increase his expenses and, possibly, get more of an insight into Rania's situation. In actual fact, he could make out that he was helping Othman in his quest to expose his old buddy and make some money in the process. He would have to be careful how he was going to approach Othman and, indeed, what he was going to say to him. Othman was clever and would soon conclude, especially when he realised the case was not going to be resurrected, that MI5 may be on to him. Othman knew the set up as he'd been involved in the Rob Williams case – once the government were out of the equation, the MI5, through 'dubious means' would step in. On hearing from himself, Othman may immediately jump to this conclusion and be less then cooperative. Thomas thought to himself. He had to get Othman on his side and allay any suspicions – the James Nathan scam, if worked properly, might just be the way to achieve this.

He parked his car in the underground car park and took the lift to the tenth floor. On entering his flat he immediately sensed a presence. Someone else was in his apartment. He checked the lounge but no one was there. There was no one in the kitchen. Was he imagining things? He heard a rustling coming from the bedroom and took his gun out of the holster. He stood by the door which was slightly ajar.

'Whoever's in there better come out as my gun is loaded.'

'Ooh I hope it is Thomas. I'm all for playing dirty.'

Thomas relaxed. He recognised the voice. It was Samantha. He walked into the room. She was kneeling on the bed completely naked.

'Well don't just stand there, are you going to use that gun or is it just for show?'

After fifteen minutes of frantic love-making the two of them rested under the bed covers.

'It's been a long time Tom, why haven't you been calling me?'

'You know what it's like Sam. Just don't get the time.'

'Well I've got needs and you ain't fulfilling them.'

'I thought I just did?'

'That's only part of it. I'm in my thirties and the clock's ticking. When are you going to make an honest woman out of me?'

'Don't push me Sam. Let me sort out work first.'

'You always say that. I can't wait around forever.'

'I know, I know. Do you want a drink?'

'Go on then.'

Samantha Wilson worked as PA to the Head of MI5 and had been seeing Thomas for the last two years. Their relationship, in essence, was based on sex and not much else. There was little pillow talk about work and although she commanded an influential position, the managers kept her out of the intrigue. She provided administrative support to the Head and that was it. She didn't have access to confidential files and wasn't involved in top secret activity – whether in a clerical capacity or any other capacity. She organised the Head's diary, booked his flights and, occasionally supported him at social functions. She was also a 'sex worker' and made a nice little living out of the many rampant operatives who wanted to carry out their sexual fantasies with no strings attached. This is how Thomas and Sam got together initially – he paid her at first but after a few dinner dates decided a payment for such services was unnecessary. Sam on the other hand continued her private trade and Thomas was okay with the arrangement – after all he didn't want a long term commitment. She, however, was beginning to change her views and, now that she'd achieved her ambitions – house, money in the bank etc., was looking to 'settle down', or so she thought.

Samantha had dyed red hair, piercing green eyes, thick red lips and a perfect figure. Of course having a perfect figure means different things to different people. For Thomas, however, it meant a 40 inch G bra cup and a rear the size of Blackpool! Her facial features were regular and not unattractive, although she could not be considered a classic beauty. In a sense she was every young man's dream – sexy, approachable, accommodating and discreet. Add that to the fact she had a repertoire that included the entire spectrum of sexual activity from domination to 'swinging from the chandeliers' or similar antics, and it was no wonder that every young operative (sometimes female) drooled at the mouth when she put on an innocent show in the office! Samantha gave the impression that she was 'easy' and not too bright, however the latter was not the case – she'd received a first at Oxford in languages and had plans to achieve celebrity status before the age of forty! Her first novel – 'Men in High Places' was a fictitious thriller based on the frailties of men. The book had been well received having been accessed by over twenty thousand subscribers on the internet. Samantha Wilson was a name to remember.

Thomas returned with two large gin and tonics and said:

'Look Sam, I've got to make a phone call. I'll be five minutes. Don't go away.'

He went into the kitchen and dialled Othman's number.

'Hi Inspector Othman. Thomas Develt.'

'Hi Thomas. I remember you well and not in a good way. What do you want?'

'Oh don't be like that. Believe it or not I'm here to help you.'

'I don't believe you, but go on.'

'The reason I'm phoning is personal and has nothing to do with work. You may know my old school chum James Nathan, Senior Oncologist at the UCH. I say he is an old school chum, but that's not really the case. I believe he's involved with some sort of scam concerning a friend of yours – Magda Ishmail. He's given me his side of the story but it doesn't stack up. I'm wondering what you can tell me about this charlatan so I can get this guy behind bars. Let me tell you straight Othman I had no idea you were in the country and only found out when this clown phoned me. He told me about Magda and mentioned your name. Small world isn't it? Anyway, to cut a long story short, he wants me to get you off his tail. He thinks I can threaten you in some way – get you deported or employ contractors to bump you off. Of course, when he said all this I realised he was into a scam and told him I couldn't touch you in any way and he'd have to fight his own corner. In fairness, he may be able to prove he's squeaky clean because of his eminence in the medical fraternity. He could just argue that the treatment your friend is receiving is the best possible treatment in the cir-cumstances. Few people stand up to professional medical opinion as you know. So really, what I'm asking is what've you got to prove his guilt?'

'I've got enough proof to prompt a full scale enquiry.'

'What's that?'

'Various photos of papers.'

'Would you be prepared to share them with me? You've got nothing to lose. I have more influence in this country than you, so I'd be doing you a favour. By the way what's happening to Magda now?'

'She's being seen by another doctor.'

'Good. Can we meet somewhere?'

'Why should I trust you Thomas? I know you left your colleague for dead in the Rob Williams case, probably because your boss told you to get rid to avoid his embarrassment?'

Thomas ignored this remark and said:

'No one can be trusted Othman, but what harm would it do for you to disclose what you've got. Besides I'll deny leaving her for dead. I'll just say I panicked. The government will not want to resurrect the Rob Williams case so I'm safe. However, you're not.'

'What do you mean?'

'I get to hear things. I know a debate's going on about whether to resurrect the Rania Hakim case and I've been told that won't be good for her or, indeed, you.'

'Bullshit.'

'Bullshit or no bullshit, if you can help me out with the Nathan case I'll use my influence to stop the case being resurrected.'

'I don't believe you.'

'Fine, then watch this space. Do you really want to put your whole career on the line? Be sensible man. Tell me what you've got on Nathan and all your troubles will be over. Now where can we meet?'

'Okay I'll see you in *The Ship Tavern* behind Holborn Underground at 3.30 pm tomorrow.'

'Good. See you then.'

Othman didn't believe a word Thomas had said but saw no reason why he couldn't disclose the papers he had on Nathan. He quickly phoned Rania and explained the situation advising her to be alert. He told her that he believed the Home Office would not be resurrecting the case and that she had nothing to fear from this perspective. However, it seemed a bit of a coincidence that Thomas DeVelt should show his face so soon after the threats made by Nigel Francis. As usual, he smelt a rat and told Rania that she must assume that the government has handed over the case to MI5. From now, she must be careful and ensure she's always in the company of others. Meanwhile, he would figure out their next move – which may, of course be a quick exit out the country. They arranged to meet the following evening.

Samantha had listened to Thomas's conversation and was intrigued. It looked like she was not going to have a future with him so she had nothing to lose. She didn't care much for him in any case. What she heard gave her a great idea for her next novel. She just might play the undercover agent game and follow her lover tomorrow. She knew *The Ship Tavern* very well and felt strangely mischievous.

CHAPTER SEVENTEEN

Othman was beginning to think that his UK trip was becoming a complete disaster. He was fond of Rania and wanted to see her again but, with this murder hanging over her head, he felt any relationship would be destined for failure. In any case, she had never showed any real interest in him and undoubtedly, even if she did, he would always be second best to Rob Williams. However, he did have some allegiance to her and, whether he liked it or not, he had set her up to take revenge on Rob's death. He felt responsible for her now and decided that he must protect her at all costs.

And then there was poor old Magda who had almost certainly been the victim of a medical scam. Thankfully he'd arranged for another specialist to see her at the Royal Marsden and, hopefully, further tests would show that the cancer is not so advanced as advised by Gustav and Nathan. Perhaps, if this were the case, she could fly back to Cairo for the standard treatment. Either that or have her operation and follow up at the Marsden – he had the funds so why not?

All in all, it had all gone wrong. They had been the victims of corrupt systems – both governmental and medical. But now it was time to stand his ground. Firstly, he had to protect Rania and secondly, he had to expose Gustav and Nathan – he couldn't rely on DeVelt to do that because, despite all that'd been said, they were old university buddies and, apart from a pay-out to keep quiet, DeVelt wouldn't expose an old mate. That's the assumption in any event. Of course, in his case, he'd been badly let down by an old mate in the guise of Inspector Nigel Francis who, incidentally, had gone very quiet recently and was unlikely to make a reappearance – or, at least, hopefully not.

He made his way to the tavern and parked himself in an empty corner. He'd wait for Thomas before ordering any drinks and decided to browse through the documents to remind himself of the evidence – a note confirming stage one cancer; a note to confirm an operation; a note from Gustav to Nathan; specimen results and a breakdown in costs differentiating standard from advanced treatments. These were copies of the photos he'd taken and were enough, as far as Othman was concerned, to instigate an enquiry. Just as his thoughts moved to Rania, in came the bustling Thomas Develt. A big man but not fat. Tall and smart sporting some kind of club tie which was pinned to his white shirt. He was not completely bald but his ginger hair had been cropped making him look like an ex con made good in the gangster world.

'Hi Othman want a drink?'

'No thanks, just make this short.'

'Okay, what have you got for me?'

Othman handed over a brown envelope. Thomas read the contents and expressed his interest. He got up and walked out the pub. He went a few yards down the alleyway and hid himself in a small shop which allowed him to see all those exiting the pub. He waited. After about five minutes Othman came out and took a right towards Holborn Underground. Thomas followed him until he reached a hotel in Russell Square. Othman entered the hotel and collected his keys from reception. Thomas made a note of the name and address and went back to his office. He hadn't noticed Samantha who had cheekily observed his movements from the moment he'd left the pub holding a brown envelope.

Later that day he phoned Nathan and told him about the documents. In the light of these disclosures he demanded £20,000 to be deposited into his account by 12.00 the next day. Provided this transaction was made, he would keep quiet about Nathan's dubious practices and deal with Othman. Nathan agreed thinking that this was his only way out. After all they were old buddies and this was all part of business.

The transaction was made the following day and Thomas considered his strategy. He was in no hurry to kill Othman so that side of his plan could wait. Accordingly, he could concentrate his efforts on Rania.

⸓ ⸓

Othman rang Rania and arranged to see her that evening as agreed. They met in an Indian restaurant off Tottenham Court Road. He told her about Thomas DeVelt.

'Look Rania, I expect the worse from this guy, so be on your guard. Better still get out the country.'

'I don't want to just yet Othman. Everything's gone quiet since my last encounter with Nigel Francis and I'd rather stick around.'

'Well, don't say I didn't warn you. Thomas could pounce at any time and I can't be with you 24/7.'

'I know that Othman and I appreciate your concern. The fact of the matter is that I feel in better spirits. I don't know why... but things have gone quiet and I'm more optimistic about the future. As I said I don't really know why. I must admit that at the moment I'm quite happy working in London and find the job at the museum very fascinating. I really don't want to leave – not yet anyway.'

'Okay, but be careful and don't take risks. Sit tight for the next few weeks and we'll take it from there. Now, what do you want to eat?'

CHAPTER EIGHTEEN

The next few weeks were quiet and it seemed that things had settled down. Othman hadn't heard from DeVelt or Francis and was able to concentrate his efforts on supporting the Ishmails. Rania became more and more involved in the activities of the museum and struck up a decent relationship with the professor who'd become a friend as well as a colleague. They bounced ideas off each other and were tasked with developing the Greek theme with a view to increasing revenue. After much debate and laughter, the professor came up with the idea of re-enacting the war between Greece and Persia, having seen the film 'The 300 Spartans' while inebriated one

Saturday afternoon! Accordingly, the professor went to great lengths to sell his idea to the powers that be in several presentations taking place over a number of days in the conference room. He would begin:

'The Battle of Thermopylae took place in 480BC between an alliance of Greek city-states, led by King Leonidas of Sparta and the Persian Empire of Xerxes over the course of three days, during the second Persian invasion of Greece. The main battle took place in a narrow pass of Thermopylae known as 'The Hot Gates'. And end:

'So ladies and gentlemen, this could be a new venture for the museum in the field of battle re-enactment; a field which will attract and educate the public; a field which will promote the museum in the 21st Century, and a field which could pro-duce more revenue and thereby benefit us all. I rest my case.'

The British Museum accepted the professor's idea of staging a mock battle on the ground floor commemorating the exploits of the 300 Spartans and, at the same time, providing details of the events leading up to this skirmish. Of course, there would be visual displays of costumes, weapons and other paraphernalia used at the time, as well as a docu-mentary running alongside a video show. The spec-tacle would complement the Greek Exhibition which had been a great success and was likely to continue for some months. The museum felt it would be a great crowd puller and could keep costs down by using volunteers within their own staff establishment. It would run for a week and the ground floor would be rearranged to accommodate the whole show.

As luck would have it, Rania was appointed project manager with Professor Lear as her advisor. The professor, of course, was ecstatic about the show, firstly because it was his idea, secondly, he would be working with his beloved Rania and, thirdly, he was in the running to play King Leonidas - although he was probably far too old to play the part. However, the thing was, the vast majority of people shied away from the main roles preferring to hide behind army ranks in an attempt to avoid public scrutiny – and total embarrassment. So the professor with his flowing white hair, Errol Flynn moustache and natural flair for dramatics, was the one and only candidate. A young and dashing student of Egyptology was prepared to play the role of Xerxes.

Costumes and weapons were quickly designed to reflect the period and the mock 'Hot Gates' were constructed in an area designated on the ground floor. Adverts were placed in most of the papers and the event was given a special mention on the six o'clock news. Tickets would cost £25 per adult and £15 per child and the occasion was so well promoted that it was a complete sell out.

Rania and the professor worked frantically in the days leading up to the premier and proved to be excellent directors when it came to the dress rehearsals. The programme would consist of an initial introduction on the big screen, followed by a brief light show with ancient music, setting the scene for short speeches by King Leonidas and Xerxis. There would then be a re-enactment of the various confrontations showing how the Greeks used various military tactics to defend their position, interrupted at the appropriate times by the video show with supporting dialogue. The finale, of course, would be the total slaughter of the entire Spartan army by an array of arrows cleverly presented in silhouette form on a white background. Health and safety regulations prevented the use of real arrows in re-enacting this mass killing! The video show would then conclude the event by describing the aftermath and the developments following the war. Apart from the historical and archaeological aspects of the show, a general theme running through the entire production was the human need for unshackled freedom and democracy – as opposed to slavery.

After a number of dress rehearsals, the first public showing took place on a Monday with the last scheduled for the following Friday. Everything went well and by Wednesday the performance was the 'talk of the town.'

Thomas DeVelt took his seat in the middle of the third row having bought a ticket following the press releases for Wednesday's performance. He was unrecognisable having grown a beard and dyed his hair black. Such a disguise wasn't really necessary as Rania had never seen him before, but Othman would have described him so it was best to take no chances. The show lasted for about ninety minutes. When it finished he decided to have a look round the Museum. He found out the whereabouts of Rania's department and located the exit by which she would most likely leave the premises. He hung around outside and waited. At around about 6.00 pm she exited the building and made her way to Holborn underground. He followed her to Barnes Station. He would execute his plan tomorrow.

CHAPTER NINETEEN

Surprisingly during the lead up to the show, including various rehearsals, Rania and Professor Angus Lear became quite close. This astounded Rania as, up to then, she'd thought of him as a buffoon! However, she got to know him better during this short period of time and, although he was eccentric, he was very kind and understanding. She learned how to handle his banter and decided that, at the end of the day, he was harmless. He was intelligent and, when he got going on his subject, inspirational. He was in his fifties and looked a bit unusual, but behind the hair and moustache lay a very handsome man. This didn't have much effect on Rania as she preferred intelligent kind men to good looking ignorant ones. There was something very attractive about an intelligent gentleman with a few grey hairs. The other thing, of course, was that he cared for her and his care was genuine. He would buy her a rose at least twice a week and although she didn't take much notice at the beginning, she began warming to the idea and missed this treat if he happened to forget to buy such a flower on any particular day.

They had coffee on a regular basis and she found herself laughing with him rather than rebuking him for his silly behaviour. She began looking forward to their meetings and soon she was accompanying him down to the museum's staff restaurant. Eventually, he asked her out for dinner and she agreed. They had a great time together and at the end of the evening they kissed.

Rania felt alive again and a bit shocked. How could she have fallen for an old professor type? On the other hand, why not? They had a lot in common. He wasn't that old and, when all was said and done, he was charming. A mature, intelligent, handsome, funny English gentleman. What else could a girl ask for?

On Thursday's performance Rania invited Angus to her flat in Barnes. The other two girls were away and she wanted to show off her cooking skills. Angus agreed and once they were seated together on the underground, they held hands. They were oblivious to the crowds as they discussed the day's performance, how well it had gone and how well Angus had portrayed the great King Leonidas! Tongue in cheek of course – Angus always bragged about his great achievements with a twinkle in his eye as he knew he was far from great. They discussed archaeology, history, films, the universe, and their conversations always flowed with no awkward silences. They were natural together. He reminded her of Rob.

Eventually they arrived at Barnes Station and the evening was getting dark. Arm in arm they walked through the 'country lanes' leading to the main part of town. They were engrossed in conversation, oblivious to the noise of the traffic and unaware that someone was following them. They entered a small 'secret' path which led to the back of Barnes Pond. This part of the journey, with the light quickly fading, was potentially dangerous for any lone walker who'd been targeted for attack. The pathway was lined with trees and bushes but was only yards away from a quiet road. Rania never gave her safety a second thought as she was with Angus who offered security and companionship. On other nights, she would tend to quicken her pace and be on her guard until she reached the pond which was situated in an open area for all to see.

Meanwhile Thomas DeVelt, dressed in black leathers, manoeuvred his motorbike into a small clearing off the road and attached a silencer to his Beretta 92FS firearm. He'd tracked the couple from the moment they'd left the British Museum. He'd then driven down to Barnes Station and waited on his motor bike behind a tree opposite the exit. When he spotted them he jumped on his bike and parked some four hundred metres from the station. Equipped with his gun he followed them until they reached the 'secret' path. He put on his balaclava and stalked them until they were in the densest part where the path was surrounded by woods. It was now or never – there was no one else around. He had to act fast. He got ahead of them and waited. Rania stopped.

'Wait a minute Angus. Did you hear that?'

'What?'

'I thought I heard something in the bushes...a rustling sound.'

'Can't hear a ...'

Just at that moment a black figure pounced out of the bushes. Angus dived in front of Rania and as he did so was shot in the stomach and chest. Both Angus and Rania fell to the floor. Thomas took aim at Rania's head but Angus rose up and grabbed his legs. This put him off his aim and his shot whistled through the trees.

'Run Rania, get out of here' Angus shouted. He pushed her away. Rania staggered towards the trees and felt a sudden pain in her leg. She'd been shot. She made it to the small road and screamed. Thomas followed her and took aim. She lurched into the road and was lit up by the headlights of a passing car. There was a screeching of brakes as the driver swerved to avoid her. Thomas fired again but this time the bullet found her neck. That's it, Thomas thought and returned to the woods. Angus was lying on the floor crying desperately for Rania. Thomas reloaded his gun and shot him twice in the head. He ran to his motorbike and made off in the direction of Putney High Street. Job done he said to himself.

The driver got out of his car and saw blood flow from a small hole in Rania's neck. He bound the wound with his scarf and bundled her into his car. Rania became drowsy as she lay on the back seat, drifting in and out of consciousness.

'Hold on.' The driver said. 'I'll get you to a hospital. Just hold on. You're going to be fine.'

'Angus, what about Angus?' Rania cried.

'Don't worry. I need to get you to a hospital.'

'Stop. We can't go without Angus.'

'We have to, otherwise you'll die. Now hold on.'

Rania woke up in Charing Cross Hospital. She had all sorts of tubes coming out of her nose and mouth. Her neck and leg were heavily bandaged. She couldn't move and cried out for a nurse. The pain in her leg was excruciating and her vision was blurred.

She noticed figures rush to her side and felt a needle go into her arm. She must've dozed off because when she came to her senses she saw Othman standing at the end of her bed.

'How are you?' he asked.

'Never felt better ' she joked. 'Thank God the pain's gone.'

'Good.'

'How long have I been here?'

'Oh, a couple of days. It was touch and go for a time as you'd lost so much blood.'

'How did you find me?'

'They found my number in your purse.'

'What about Angus?'

Othman hesitated and then said:

'He's dead I'm afraid. Whoever killed him made sure of the job.'

There was a pause and Rania's eyes welled up.

'He died saving me. We were getting on so well together.'

'I know, I know, I'm so terribly sorry.' Othman held her hand. There was another pause. 'What happened?' asked Othman, ignoring her tears.

'I don't want to speak now. Leave me alone Othman. I can't believe Angus is dead. I want to sleep.'

Rania turned over and sobbed. She was desolate. Eventually she fell asleep and Othman decided to return later in the day. At around 4.00 pm he returned:

'Can you talk now Rania? What happened?'

Rania stirred and became lucid. Her eyes stared in front of her and her mind focussed on the past events:

'It was so quick. A figure came out of the trees with a gun. Next thing I knew Angus dived in front of me. He pushed me away and told me to run. I did. All I can remember after that was a pain in my leg and being lit up by headlamps.'

'Well the police will want to speak to you soon but I suspect a Mr Thomas DeVelt is behind all this. As you know, he works for MI5 and has probably been told to silence both you and me. I've told you all this before.'

'But why?'

'Well, nothing's been released in the press about us because, I suspect, the government doesn't want a resurrection of the case. Questions were bound to be asked about Rob Williams and the politicians won't want to do anything to provoke further enquiries. On the other hand, they have probably concluded that you did kill Sir Michael Wilkinson and want you out the way. Of course, they don't want to be associated with any assassination so called upon MI5 to do their dirty work. I may be completely wrong, but that's the way I'm looking at it. DeVelt contacted me a few days ago asking questions about Nathan the oncologist. He told me this had nothing to do with anything else but his contacting me was a bit of a coincidence following my old school mate's involvement in affairs. That's why I warned you to be careful.'

Rania started crying. She was shocked by the whole event but her heart sunk further when she realised how great a man Professor Angus Lear turned out to be. First there was Dr Rob Williams who'd died in her arms, and now there was Angus who'd died saving her. Both men were heroes, both men were dead. Both men she'd loved.

'Look, I'm sorry Rania for how things have turned out... but you're still alive and you have a life to lead. Things must go on. I'm not going to leave your side again. I'm staying with you until we sort this all out. Now, you're tired. Go to sleep. I'll sit in that chair over there.'

Just as both of them were dozing off Inspector Nigel Francis entered the room:

'Good evening Ms Hakim. How are you?' Nigel didn't notice Othman sitting in the chair in the corner.

Rania was livid:

'You've got a nerve turning up here. After all the pain you've caused, you have the audacity to enquire about my health? You must be joking.'

'I know and I'm sorry for what happened in the past. But the thing is this; your colleague has been murdered and I've been assigned to investigate the case. We both better get used to the situation. I'm sorry for what I did and I'm sorry for the death of your friend, but now we have to move forward and catch the killer.'

'Hi Nigel' Othman piped up 'remember me? I'm your best mate or, at least, was your best mate until you tried to blackmail me – you git.'

'Hi Othman. Look I'm sorry for what I did but haven't got the time to put on a lengthy grovelling show. We've got to track down this killer. You'd better tell me what's going on Miss Hakim - I'm all ears... oh, and Othman, perhaps you can help me fill in the gaps as well?'

'You're a callous bastard Inspector f..k up Francis. You know what's going on. MI5 tried to bump Rania off as the government don't want to dig up the dirt.'

'We don't know any of that Othman. I'm here to investigate the murder of Professor Angus Lear. Now, I need names, addresses, times, dates and your account of what happened, Miss Hakim.'

CHAPTER TWENTY

The headlines in *The Times* read:

**PROFESSOR KILLED IN MYSTERIOUS CIR-
CUMSTANCES**
*Around 7.00 pm Thursday 4th September 2004
Professor Angus Lear was found dead on Barnes
Common. He had been shot in the stomach, chest
and head. The professor worked for the British
Museum and was one of the country's leading
archaeologists. Inspector Nigel Francis of the
Metropolitan Police states: 'We believe a Miss
Rania Hakim was accompanying the professor at
the time of his attack. She claims that a hooded*

figure approached them while walking on a path towards her home and pointed a gun at them. The professor immediately dived in front of her and, as a consequence, was shot. She escaped with wounds to her head and neck and remains in a stable but critical condition. She is unable to identify the assailant although she believes he was a tall man dressed in black, hooded with a balaclava covering his face. She wanted to take the opportunity to thank the motorist who took her to a nearby hospital. If he had not acted so quickly Miss Hakim would have died.'

Miss Rania Hakim was a prime suspect in the Head of MI5 murder although all charges were dropped against her. The investigations continue.

Joshua Wilson-Smith, Head of MI5 flung the newspapers across the table towards Thomas DeVelt. Richard Scott, Deputy Chief Constable and the Home Secretary were sitting each side of him.

'Why didn't you finish the job Thomas? he asked.

'I thought I had sir.'

'You bungled it.'

'I'm sorry sir.'

'Sorry is not good enough' said the Home Secretary. 'You managed to kill an innocent professor but failed to achieve the objective. This is a disaster.'

'I agree Home Secretary' said Richard Scott. 'This is a disaster.'

'Look, I didn't know that the professor was going to play heroics. I picked my time. I couldn't wait. It was unfortunate he got in the way.'

'Unfortunate?' the HS asked. 'It's blatant incompetence. We've now got Rania Hakim's name in the newspapers again. It will not take a genius to realise, after reading this article, that someone wanted her out of the way. People will suspect underhand activity following the previous reports on the resurrection of the case against her.'

'But she's not dead sir?' said Thomas.

'No, but she's in the spotlight again and while she's in the spotlight able to talk, the revival of the Rob William's case is always a possibility... this whole thing has become very messy Joshua, largely due to Mr DeVelt here. What are you going to do about it?'

'Well Home Secretary, internal procedures will be applied.'

'What does that mean?'

Joshua turned to Thomas and told him he was suspended pending further enquiries. He told him to go home, sit in the garden and not to get involved in any work until he'd heard from his employers. Thomas got up and went towards the door.

'Hold up Thomas. Before you go, give me all your passes, keys and weapons. Put everything out on the table now.'

Thomas emptied his pockets and the contents of his cases and made for the exit. As he got to the door Joshua said:

'Remember your confidentiality and restraint clauses Thomas. You may be feeling bruised but keep this whole thing to yourself. Not a word to anyone. I suggest you leave the country for a few days. Go for a little holiday but keep in touch. We don't want to have to despatch an operative to sort you out do we?'

'No sir. I'll just say one thing. I'm a field operative and have to make life and death decisions on the ground. I was merely carrying out my duties in the best way I could and in the circumstances I found myself. You guys mostly sit round tables getting others to do the real work and taking the glory when things go well. You entrusted me to do your dirty work – don't forget that.'

'But that's the deal Thomas. That's the way it is. Had you been successful we would not be having this conversation. But you haven't. You killed an innocent man and failed to hit your target. Now you must suffer the consequences. I suggest you go home and think about that.'

Joshua motioned him to the door. Thomas left the room slamming the door as he did so.

'Now Joshua, back to the question. What are you going to do?' asked the Home Secretary.

Joshua looked at both gentlemen: 'Absolutely nothing... the professor was not married, didn't have kids, no brothers or sisters, no next of kin – in fact, he was a lone wolf. Nobody apart from Hakim cared about him. So who's going to sing his song? Who's going to champion his campaign? No one. Let me deal with Thomas. You, Richard carry out all your investigations but don't spend too much time on it – you haven't the resources. Just keep the papers thinking that the wheels of natural justice are turning and that once the murderer is found – due process will apply. You, Home Secretary, can reassure the Prime Minister that nothing will come of this and the press will eventually go away once it realises that there's nothing more to report. As for me, well, I'm going home.'

'Wait a minute Joshua, what about Rania Hakim and her accomplice Inspector Othman?' asked the Home Secretary.

'Well, put yourselves in their shoes. What would you do?'

'Get out of the country as soon as possible.'

'Precisely. We know their movements and we know what they're likely to do. They could still cause significant embarrassment to the government and we know that Hakim killed my honourable predecessor. They still have to be removed one way or another. But let's not panic. Let's think through our strategy.'

'I'll leave that to you Joshua. But don't involve the government. Do whatever is necessary to eliminate the resurrection of the Rob Williams case – that's all we care about. Do what you have to do.'

'Of course Home Secretary. Give my regards to your wife.'

'I will.'

The Home Secretary and Deputy Chief Constable left the room. Joshua swivelled his chair round and looked at himself in the mirror. He thought about Thomas Develt and what he was going to do about him. He needed a shave. He studied his receding hairline and the remains of his short black curls. He'd inherited his hair from his mother who had been a beautiful Jamaican lady who, at one time, sported a wonderful 'afro' hair style. His father was African American who'd divorced his mother several years ago. Joshua was educated at Eton and Oxford and was proud to be the first black Head of MI5. He was proud to be part of the establishment and saluted the picture of the Queen which hung on the wall behind him. What am I to do with Thomas, he kept asking himself. Perhaps he should give him a final chance to redeem himself. After all, he didn't want to expend any further resources. Yes, give him one more chance to kill or be killed or, hopefully, both.

PARAGRAPH
TWENTY-ONE

Thomas DeVelt was filled with bitterness and rage. He'd messed up but he despised the arrogance of his superiors – sitting there in their ivory towers – they had it so easy. He did the work, they took the glory. He'd put himself on the line and what thanks did he get? - None. All they could do was to criticise. He drank a couple of large gins and phoned Samantha.

'Hi Sam. I'm down. Come here and cheer me up.'

'But I've got work to do.'

'Well, come round as soon as you can. I've been suspended.'

'What?'

'Suspended pending further enquiries.'

'Why?'

'I can't tell you over the phone but I need your support.'

'Okay, I'll be over as soon as I can.'

Thomas had another couple of large gins and sank back in his armchair. He thought about Samantha. The drink made him lustful. He would forget about his problems by consuming excessive amounts of alcohol and indulging in a wide range of sexual activity – he joked to himself. He got lost in his fantasies and dozed off. After about 20 minutes he was awakened by a knock on the door. Thomas staggered to the hallway and let Samantha in.

'You look pissed.'

'Join me in a drink.'

'Not until you tell me what's going on.'

'There's not much to tell. I was doing my job and shot the professor by mistake. I thought I'd killed Rania but she's still alive. Now I'm taking the rap. Hung out to dry, suspended from duty and all that crap.'

'Who are these people? Are they the ones mentioned in the papers today?'

'Never mind. Have a drink.'

'No, I don't want one. You shouldn't be telling me this in any case.'

Thomas poured himself out another large gin and drank it in one gulp.

'I've got to tell someone. You should support me. I've paid you enough in the past. Now, come here.'

Thomas grabbed her arm.

'I think I'd better go. You're in no fit state to do anything.'

'Stay. You might be able to help me. You can change Joshua's mind. You can convince him to give me another chance.'

'This has nothing to do with me. If I did that I'd lose my job.'

'Then offer him your tits. Do what you do best.'

'I've had enough. I'm going.'

'No you're not.'

Thomas changed his mood from drunk to predator. He grabbed Samantha by the arm and dragged her into the bedroom. She screamed and lashed out. He ignored her and ripped her blouse open. She struggled to get free but Thomas was too strong. She told him to stop but he didn't. He slid her knickers off and parted her legs. She closed her eyes and told him not to hurt her - but he forced himself into her. Within seconds he came and told her to go. She scrambled into the bathroom and locked the door. Thomas had another drink and fell backwards on to the bed. He began snoring. Samantha crept out of the loo, stuffed her knickers in her bag and made for the exit.

She was just about to open the front door when a hand clasped her ankle. She screamed.

'Let go.'

'Not until I've done with you' Thomas shouted as he got up from the floor. 'Don't tell anyone about this, do you understand? Nothing happened here to-day. I didn't tell you anything about my mission and we didn't have sex.'

'We didn't have sex – you raped me.'

Thomas smacked her around the mouth and pushed her against the door.

'Listen whore, nothing happened here. I've killed before and I won't hesitate to kill you. Do you understand? Keep your mouth shut.'

'I understand, now let me go.'

Thomas released her and she ran out of his apartment crying. She drove to the nearest police station and made a statement to the sergeant on duty. She played back the recording she'd made from the moment she'd entered Thomas's apartment. The Sergeant listened with interest.

'I think I'd better talk to my boss. Thomas DeVelt from the MI5 you said?'

'That's right. I want him dead.'

'Now now Miss Wilson, that talk is not going to get us anywhere. Just wait here and I'll get the right people on the case straightaway.'

CHAPTER TWENTY-TWO

After a few days Rania was released from hospital and she and Othman went back to her flat in Barnes. Her apartment consisted of one large bedroom, a lounge and kitchen diner. It was part of a large Georgian house in which two friends also resided. They each had their own front door but, in practice, they spent a lot of time with each other, sharing their apartments on a communal basis. Rania's lounge was tastefully decorated. She had a large sofa facing a gigantic bay window which looked out to the pond. In the two corners were matching armchairs which were used only when she had visitors. The polished wooden floor was partly covered by a magnificent Persian rug which depicted exotic birds flying around willow trees set against a mountainous backdrop. The wool was stained a deep burgundy and the edges were lined with tassels which had been neatly combed out.

A coffee table was positioned between the sofa and the bay window and supported what looked like a number of miniature archaeological pieces, possibly from China. They were small figurines of emperors and soldiers, each with swept back hair tied in bows, and each wearing long gowns with sashes surrounding their torsos. Such features could just be made out as the ravages of time had taken their toll leaving the figures incomplete in some places.

The walls had been painted white with pictures displayed on one side of the room. On the other was a large mirror encased in a beautifully carved wooden frame painted matt white which did little to contrast with the surrounding wall. Nevertheless, the mirror was distinctive and served as a prominent feature for the room as well as making the latter appear bigger than it really was.

On entering the lounge Othman saw himself and Rania, and, indeed, the whole room itself reflected in the mirror and felt, for one, moment, that he was looking into a further room beyond the lounge.

'Wow' he said 'this is impressive. You've really gone to town with the decor Rania.'

'Thank you. I like to keep things simple.'

'What's the rest of the apartment like?'

'I'll show you.'

Rania did a quick tour of the flat and offered Othman a cup of coffee. They sat in the lounge and talked about their predicament:

'Angus didn't deserve to die in all this, and although I would love to exact revenge on his murderer I don't think I would get away with it again.'

'Don't even go there Rania 'said Othman. 'It's clear they're out to get you and possibly me but they don't want the Rob Williams case resurrected. Thomas DeVelt or whoever tried to kill you, bungled the job and it's unlikely that they'll use the same operative again. We have to assume we're still under serious threat and that while we're alive we're never going to be safe in the UK.'

'So what do we do?'

'We have to get out. Go back to Cairo and hope for the best.'

'What about your friends?'

'I think they're in safe hands, as far as Magda's treatment is concerned, but anyone associated with me or you are at risk. Let's face it Rania we both knew that MI5 were behind Rob's killing and the government know that we know. Add that to the fact that you murdered the Head of MI5, with me as your accomplice, and you have a situation that won't be tolerated by the authorities. We may not even be safe in Egypt so we may have to lie low in Sudan or even Baghdad.'

'Forget about Baghdad Othman, that city is being bombed beyond recognition.'

'Yes, of course. We may have to think further afield like the States, Canada or France. Do you speak French?'

'I can get by, but I'm not fluent.'

'The other option is to do nothing. Sit it out and see what happens. It may be, with the bungled attempt on your life, the authorities may 'let sleeping dogs lie'. They won't want to waste further resources on this case and, of course, won't want to attract further attention.'

'But we'll remain in a constant state of fear and anxiety.'

'Not forever Rania, I assure you. If you don't mind, I'd like to stay here and watch over you. I can use the sofa?'

'You don't have to Othman but I would appreciate it.'

'Also, I want to send a complaint letter to the BMA, with a copy to the Chief Constable, regarding the scam that's going on between Nathan and Gustav. That's not your problem of course but I may as well get on to that straight away while we figure out what we're going to do.'

'Okay, but copy me in on everything, just in case something happens to you. In the meantime, let me prepare some food. There's some wine in the fridge.'

⇥ ⇤

Thomas DeVelt was woken by his phone. It was the Head of MI5:

'Thomas, you are in the shit. Don't say a word. Just listen. I had the Deputy Chief Constable on the phone last night telling me that a certain Samantha Wilson aka my PA was raped and assaulted by your good self. Is this true?'

'I don't remember sir. I was pissed.'

'Not a good answer Thomas. I'm going to assume you did. Samantha is on sick leave helping the police with their enquiries and you are suspended having failed to meet your objective. You are a liability Thomas but I'm not going to 'hang you out to dry' just yet.'

'What do you mean?'

'I will sort Samantha out and keep the police off your tail. In return sort out Hakim and Othman. This is your last chance. You've got nothing to lose. You're in the realms of desperation. Do a good job and I'll keep Samantha sweet. She'll drop the charges and the police won't hound you. If you cock up again, not only will you lose your job, but you'll be banged up for a minimum of five years. Do you understand what I'm saying Thomas?'

'Of course I do.'

'Good, now sober up and finish the job.'

'Can I speak to Samantha. I want to apologise.'

'Don't be an idiot. Of course not. Leave her to me. Once she sees the bigger picture, I'm sure she'll understand.'

Joshua put the phone down and rang Samantha. He told her that Thomas was pissed and didn't know what he was doing – which didn't make any difference as far as Samantha was concerned – and told her to hold off until Thomas had completed his mission. He explained that Hakim and Othman were well known terrorists and had murdered the former Head of MI5. The government had instructed that they must be brought to justice and that Thomas was the best man for the job.

'So what I'm saying Sam is this. I know you've got a good case against that dickhead but for the sake of national security I'm asking you to hold back. Once he's done his bit for Britain, you can unleash your fury.'

'And what's in it for me Josh?'

'A very respectable pay increase.'

'How much?'

'15%.'

'Make it 25% as a tax free one off lump sum, in my account by tomorrow.'

'Consider it done.'

Joshua then phoned the Deputy Chief Constable and explained the situation to him. Richard Scott, normally a weak man, explained that he couldn't hold off investigations as a crime had clearly been committed. There was clear evidence of rape and assault. Joshua explained the wider picture and told him that Samantha had promised to back off – for the time being.

'This is very difficult Joshua. I would need something from the Chief or even the Home Secretary to sanction this. I can't just stop enquiries into a clear charge of rape. What would my men think?'

'I don't care about your men and, if truth be told, nor do you. You won't be stopping enquires, just holding them off. I'll get the Home Secretary to write you a letter. In fact, better still, I'll type it myself and sign it on his behalf. I'm sure we've got some government headed paper somewhere. You do this one favour for me Dickie and your promotion is assured. I will write a personal letter to the Home Secretary advising him that you were extremely co-operative in governmental affairs and that you went beyond the call of duty in dealing with matters of national security. The government love to have obedient chief constables able to demonstrate servitude at their beck and call.'

'I'm not sure whether that's a compliment or not Joshua. But I'll take it in good faith. After all, my country must come first, whatever the circumstances.'

'Good man. There'll be a cheque in the post for good measure, so 'keep your hounds at bay.' Any cock up on your part will result in the very opposite of promotion, and I don't mean demotion.'

'What do you mean then?'

'Termination.'

CHAPTER
TWENTY-THREE

Othman drafted the following letter to the Chief Constable of the Metropolitan Police copied to the British Medical Association, Chief Executive of the UCH, Chief Executive of The Royal Marsden and the Health Secretary.

Dear Sirs

Complaint against Messrs James Nathan and Maximilian Gustav with regard to patient Magda Ishmail patient number 67359

I am the beneficiary for patient Magda Ishmail who was originally diagnosed with stage one breast

cancer in Cairo. She could not afford private treatment so was placed on a waiting list for surgical
removal of the tumour. I advised that she should
not wait and offered to be her beneficiary for private
treatment.

Accordingly, she visited Mr Maximilian Gustav
in Cairo. He is a cancer specialist. He advised her
that her cancer was advanced and unusual and
that her chances of survival would increase if she
had specialised treatment in London.

He advised his colleague in London, Mr James
Nathan, that Mrs Ishmail would need advanced
treatment which would cost nearly £300,000.

On arrival at Mr Nathan's clinic she under-
went a number of tests. These included urine and
stool assessments. He advised Mrs Ishmail that the
results revealed blood in both specimens and that
he would adjust the chemotherapy accordingly. He
then applied aggressive chemotherapy for advanced
breast cancer.

Subsequent evidence showed that both tests were
clear and revealed no traces of blood.

It is my belief that Mrs Ishmail would be
charged at the higher rate for advanced treatment,
i.e. £300,000 when only the standard treatment
was necessary. Either he was going to subject her to
this treatment and charge at the higher rate or apply
the standard treatment at the lower rate but charge
at the higher rate.

The implication of this arrangement is that both Messrs Nathan and Gustav are involved in a scam whereby they pocket the difference between standard and advanced treatments.

The relevant papers are attached as evidence.

Needless to say, Mrs Ishmail was withdrawn from Mr Nathan's clinic and transferred to the Royal Marsden. This hospital confirmed stage one cancer and the tumour has been successfully removed.

As a consequence of this malpractice, Mrs Ishmail has had to undergo needless chemo-therapy sessions, using the most potent of drugs, under the direction of Mr Nathan. She will there-fore be pursuing her case through the courts at the appropriate time with a view to substantial compensation.

Please investigate this case as a matter of ur-gency which, up to now, has not been made known to the press but, depending on your response, will be an option which I will pursue on Mrs Ishmail's behalf.

I look forward to hearing from you soon and certainly within the next five days – otherwise I will make a full disclosure to the press.
Yours sincerely
Chief Inspector Othman of the Cairo Police Force

Othman copied this letter and all the evidence to Rania providing her with the contact details of the Ishmails. He also posted a copy to the Ishmails for safe keeping.

'Right, I'm now going to post these packages to the big boys and hope I get a reaction. I'll be about half an hour. I'll send them by first class recorded delivery. Stay put Rania and don't open your door to anyone.'

'Okay Othman, be careful.'

Meanwhile Thomas Develt had been licking his wounds in his apartment alongside preparing for the final showdown. He'd changed his strategy some-what because he'd had a call from James Nathan asking whether Othman had been dealt with. Nathan reminded him that he'd paid him handsomely for his services and expected an old school mate to do the business. Nathan also told him that he was getting jittery because he'd heard through the grapevine that Mrs Ishmail's operation for stage one had been successful with no advancement of the disease. Fortunately the medical fraternity at his level were all buddies and none of them would ever dream of blowing the whistle. Add this to the fact that Mrs Ishmail was unlikely to raise the issue as she dreaded any kind of confrontation with authority, and the situation appeared to be contained. However, Nathan reminded Thomas that Othman was the only 'fly in the ointment' and unless he was silenced quickly he could still find himself in the mire.

Thomas concluded, therefore, that it was to their mutual benefit that Othman be silenced. He'd become a nuisance to MI5 and was clearly a threat to certain members of the medical profession. He would have to act now, and with Othman out the way Hakim would lose her body guard which would make his job that much easier. Yes, on reflection, Othman would have to go first and Rania second.

He phoned Othman's mobile but no one answered. He checked his hotel room but no one was there. It didn't take a genius to realise that he would probably be with Rania Hakim. He obtained her address from the Deputy Chief Constable who was more than willing to cooperate, and motored down to Barnes.

He parked his motorbike in a side road and walked towards the pond. He spotted Rania's house and sat on a bench on the other side of the road. He positioned himself so that it would be impossible for anyone to spot him from the house. He would sit, wait and observe. After about 30 minutes, there was movement around the front door. It was Othman. He was walking towards the high street with a package in his hand. Thomas followed him to the corner of the road. There were too many people around to mount a full blown attack. In any case, he preferred the darkness and, at that point in time, it was far from dark. On the other hand, he didn't want to waste any time and the quicker he made a killing the quicker he would get into his boss's good books.

Meanwhile Othman entered the post office and searched around for his wallet. He couldn't find it. He must have left it in the flat. He searched his pockets for change – nothing. He'd have to go back. Othman left the post office and trotted back towards the flat. Thomas noticed Othman running towards the pond. He's forgotten something, he thought. Now's his chance. He could creep up behind him as he opens the front door...he'd have to act fast. There'll be people around but they'd be too shocked to do anything. In any case, that was what he was banking on.

Rania gazed out of her front window and saw Othman hurrying back with the package in his hands. At the same time she saw a dark figure in leathers and balaclava cross the road towards her house. Who's that? she thought - he looks familiar. And then the details of her attack came flooding back. Of course, big man in leathers - her attacker! She frantically tapped the window hoping she would attract attention and he would retreat. He didn't. From that point, everything seemed to be in slow motion – Othman trotting towards the front door, the attacker negotiating the traffic while trying to keep out of public sight, and Rania, now in panic mode, racing towards the hall way which led to the front door.

Othman arrived at the door, Rania opened it and Thomas pounced causing all three to end up on the hallway floor in a heap. He flung himself on the door causing it to close and, like a darting cobra, turned and plunged his knife into Othman's leg as the latter approached him. The package he was holding went flying down the hall way. Rania grabbed Thomas around the neck but he was too strong and she was flung to the wall with such force that her head split open. Othman revived himself and mustered all his strength to fight Thomas off. He grabbed his hand and twisted it until he released the knife. The knife went hurtling down the hallway with both men diving for it. Thomas got there first and swung the knife in the direction of Othman's abdomen. He missed and while he was off balance Othman kicked him in the head with his good leg. This stunned him and for a split second he was dazed. Othman took the advantage and kicked him again. He rolled on the floor in pain. Othman dived on him and clasped his throat with both hands. Thomas made gurgling sounds as Othman's hands tightened. He desperately felt for his knife which he'd dropped while being kicked and with one last burst of energy managed to make contact with the handle. He secured a decent grip and plunged the knife into Othman's back. Othman released his grip and cried out in pain. Thomas rolled him off and was just about to administer the final blow when Rania, who had gained consciousness, plunged the pointed end of an umbrella into his neck. Unfortunately, she was still weak and the point didn't penetrate very far. He quickly turned round and punched her in the face breaking her cheekbone as he did so. Rania recoiled and slumped to the floor. Othman was lying motionless so Thomas took his knife and without hesitation cut his throat. The blood spurted on to the wooden floor, formed a pool of burgundy and spread towards the front door. Thomas kneeled down and panted. He was exhausted and couldn't move. After a couple of minutes he looked up to find the door wide open with no sign of Rania. He pocketed his knife and stumbled towards the door hoping to find Rania near at hand. She was gone. He rushed out of the house and into the traffic. Motorists screeched their brakes and blew their horns. There was pandemonium in rural Barnes as he dodged the traffic making his way towards the pond and then on to the side streets. He needed to get away. People in the street froze as he rushed past them. No one thought to stop him. No one wanted to get involved.

Meanwhile Rania, who had opened the front door – but after witnessing Othman's throat being cut - had made her way in panic towards her bathroom. On arrival she must've fainted because she couldn't remember anything until she heard the hooting of horns in the street. She rushed down the hallway and saw Othman in a pool of blood. She felt for a pulse and gave mouth to mouth. He was still alive, although his pulse was very weak. She called for an ambulance and within minutes her house was surrounded by police officers and paramedics. Inspector Francis was first on the scene. Fortunately her two friends had, by this time, arrived and were busy trying to console Rania - although this proved difficult as she was desperately trying to control the bleeding. The cut to Othman's throat was delivered in haste and had not severed the windpipe or jugular vein. This meant he had a chance, but Rania didn't know that at the time – she was sure he was dying.

Under the command of Inspector Francis, the police were ordered off the site and the paramedics told to whisk Othman off to hospital. They managed to stop the bleeding but his pulse was getting weaker. He opened his eyes and saw a friendly face. She was dressed in green, about 30 with blond hair tied tightly back revealing a smooth regal forehead and beautiful green eyes. Her skin was unblemished and her lips a crimson red. Othman thought he had died and gone to heaven. He tried to talk but the pain in his back was unbearable so he screwed his eyes and tightened his mouth to convey discomfort. She told him it wouldn't be long and administered some more oxygen and pain killer. His eyes closed and he surrendered to the sensation of floating away. The next thing he remembered was waking up in hospital in a private room facing his old university mate – Nigel Francis.

'How are you buddy?'

Othman's neck was heavily bandaged and his back was on fire, although he could tolerate the discomfort. He was more concerned about a new pain which was developing in his leg. At the end of the day none of his wounds were life threatening and, with a few pain killers, he felt sure he could discharge himself.

'Feel terrible, but what do you want?' Othman croaked with some difficulty.

'I heard about what's been going on and thought I'd come to see you.'

'What to blackmail me again?'

'Look Othman, I've come to apologise again. My behaviour has been disgraceful and I'm lucky I've not been banged up.'

'Bit late for an apology Inspector.'

'I know, but what's done is done. I've come to help.'

'What help?'

'To get you out of here.'

'And how can I trust you ever again Nigel – you've lost your way?'

'I can understand that you don't trust me. You'll just have to take my word that I want to help.'

'Go on.'

'Well, let me try to explain why I've behaved like a dickhead first.'

'This better be good Nigel.'

'Look Othman, I've become very cynical over the years working for the Met. It's different over here. It's not like Cairo.'

'How would you know?'

'I don't, I'm just guessing. Over the years things have changed. It's all paperwork and targets. While we're engaged in documentation we're not catching the bad guys. Our bosses are useless. There's no leadership. It's all political. No one wants to take responsibility. They just want to pass the buck and remain blameless. Years ago you could just clip a kid round the ear and tell them not to pinch a bag of crisps again. Job done, no paperwork and there was a good chance the kid would grow up sensibly. Nowadays, if you did that you'd get an official warning if you were lucky, or the sack if you weren't. In the end you become as bad as your managers and lose sight of what's right. You get complacent and then you get greedy.'

'Greedy for what?'

'Greedy for what you think is justice. The bosses get away with all sorts of misdemeanours and get highly paid for doing so. They abuse their positions and it's all unfair. You then lose sight of what it's all about and want a piece of the action.'

'Like bribing your best mate?'

'That's what it came to. I then got a jolt when I realised what I'd done. Just because the managers behaved badly didn't mean that I had to act in the same way. I'm totally ashamed when I think of what I've become.'

'So you're looking for atonement?' There was a pause. 'You still haven't given me a good excuse for your atrocious behaviour.'

'I know, and I don't expect you to forgive me. But you use the word atonement. Yes, I'm trying to atone myself – what else can I do? If I were a Catholic, I could just go to confession. But I'm not, so atonement is the next best thing. Call it atonement, call it repentance, call it what you like – I need to do something.'

'What made you change?'

'When I heard about Professor Lear and the attempted murder of Rania, I knew that something was very wrong – not only with individuals but with the system itself - and decided to go straight and confess my sins. I then heard about you and got myself over to the hospital as quick as I could.'

'Who have you confessed to – you're not a Catholic?'

'I know, and apart from you I haven't confessed to anyone. Having said that the PM and all his cronies knew about what I did.'

'And what did they say?'

'They said don't do it again, which, really, doesn't go far enough in terms of my redemption. They went further and told me that I would be promoted if I dropped my enquiries regarding Rania – they don't want a resurrection of the Rob Williams case.'

'I gathered that.'

'So that's when I thought the situation stank and when I reflected on my predicament I realised that, in my quest to get a name for myself in exposing Rania, I had resorted to crime or the *wrong path* as Buddhists would say. I became a poor pathetic excuse for a human being, let alone a police inspector. I was an arse hole'.

'I second that. But what now?'

'You're in danger Othman and the authorities won't stop until you're six feet under.'

'What a detective you are Nigel.'

'Seriously, I have to get you out of the country with the authorities thinking you're dead. Then that will be the end of it. I was first on the scene and...'

'But I thought you heard I was in hospital and so came down here?'

'Not exactly, when we got the call I headed up the team and was first to arrive in Barnes. You looked dead. As soon as the paramedics were ready I ordered them to cart you away. I also told the officers to get lost. I told them I would handle everything. I didn't tell anybody your name. I told the hospital that I would give them all the information as soon as I could. Rania thinks you're dead, the hospital doesn't know who you are and, with the contacts I have at the airport, I'm going to get you out of this country with everybody thinking you're dead. I haven't got much time and needless to say I'm breaking every rule in the book. That's the least I can do for my old buddy.'

'Very gallant of you, but what about Rania?'

'You'll just have to trust me on this one Othman – leave her to me. I'll get her the protection she needs and take it from there. My first priority is you. You've been seriously wounded and you're lucky not to be dead. I'm going to make a few phone calls and get you back to Cairo.'

'And say if I don't want to go?'

'You've got to go. We need you alive Othman.'

'Why me?'

'Because you stand up to the authorities while others don't bother. The police force needs heroes like you.'

'That's utter bullshit. I'm not going and that's final.'

'Fine, we'll see.'

Nigel decided to risk his arm in order to save his friend. He rang the Deputy Chief Constable and told him Inspector Othman had been murdered. He told him to inform the Home Secretary and Head of MI5. He didn't provide the details or the name of the hospital. He then rang Nick Roper from *The Sun* and gave him the same story.

He then went back to Othman's room and waited for the nurse to finish her chores. When she left he closed the door and, without warning, smothered Othman's face with a cloth that had been soaked in chloroform. Othman struggled but Nigel kept the cloth pressed down on his mouth and nose. Eventually, Othman took a breath and began to lose consciousness. After a few minutes he was out for the count. Nigel knew that when he started to regain consciousness he would feel drowsy and sick – which was just what Nigel wanted.

He'd arranged for a police car to remain outside the main entrance and, without hesitation, opened the door and pushed Othman's bed down the corridor towards the lifts. Few people noticed him and those who did thought Nigel was some kind of special hospital porter and refrained from interfering. Nigel was 'winging it' as he pushed the bed towards the main entrance. People realised that something was odd but no one did anything but looked on with anxious expressions on their faces. At last the security guards confronted him and Nigel showed his ID which stopped them in their tracks for a moment. They paused for a few seconds and then gathered around him having realised that they would be failing in their duty if they didn't investigate the situation further; but by this time Nigel could see the police car and made a mad dash for the exit. The security guards gave chase commanding Nigel to stop but it was too late – Nigel had got through the exit and wasn't waiting to hear what they had to say. Two colleagues jumped out of the car and helped Nigel get Othman into the back seat. By this time Othman was beginning to wake up, although he felt drowsy, headachy and decidedly sick.

The next thing he knew he was sitting in a plane destined for Cairo. A steward offered him the newspapers which were dated 16th September 2004. He took them and read the main story:

CHIEF INSPECTOR FROM CAIRO BRUTALLY MURDERED

Chief Inspector Othman from the Cairo Police Force was brutally murdered yesterday at around 6 pm in Barnes. The Inspector was holidaying in the UK and looking after some friends who were being treated for cancer. He was a close friend of Miss Rania Hakim who narrowly escaped a previous assault in which Professor Angus Lear was murdered. She was present when the latest murder took place and believes the killer is the same man who murdered the professor.

Both Rania Hakim and Inspector Othman were both involved in the Dr Rob Williams case in which an unknown contractor murdered him in a suburb of Cairo. One theory suggests that Dr Williams was too vocal about his opposition to the Iraq war and had to be eliminated.

In a turn of events, the Head of MI5, Sir Michael Wilkinson was subsequently murdered in an underground car park sometime last year and Miss Hakim was the prime suspect. However, all charges were dropped against her and investigations continue.

Some people now believe that MI5 may have been behind the Rob Williams killing and that Rania Hakim, his lover, took revenge on Sir Michael with Inspector Othman acting as an accomplice. MI5

*has rejected this theory and deny any involvement
in the Rob Williams case. Investigations continue.*

That bastard Francis, he thought, he's orchestrat-
ed my own death. He then turned the page and
found a small envelope. He took out a small note
which read:

*Sorry buddy for all the angst I've caused but want
you alive even though you are officially dead! Had
no choice. Had to atone. Continue to play dead. A
funeral has been arranged in Khartoum where you
will be buried alongside your father. Don't worry
about Rania. Leave her to me. Remember I've always been number one batsman so can take the in-
evitable flack. Continue to enjoy your death and
keep a low profile. I will contact you soon.*
Inspector Nigel Francis
16th September 2004

⊷⊶

Meanwhile, Rania had posted the packages which
should have gone the day before. At least that was
one thing she could do for her dead friend. Her next
job was to make contact with the Ishmails as she felt
a kind of responsibility for them, now that Othman
had died. She arranged to meet them that afternoon

despite her injuries. Her other assignment that day was to attend Angus's funeral at Highgate Cemetery, and so she put on her best black dress and best designer sun glasses, and called a cab. She was past caring about her own safety and how she looked – all those she cared for were dead – so it was just a matter of time before the next attack, which would probably be her last.

CHAPTER
TWENTY-FOUR

'I suppose you've read the papers?' asked Joshua on the phone to Thomas.

'I have sir.'

'Another cock up?'

'Not really sir, Inspector Othman is out of the way.'

'What about Hakim?

'She's next sir.'

'The problem is Thomas is that every time you make a killing, the newspapers get involved and the whole Rob Williams case is cited. It's the very thing the Government doesn't want.'

'It can't be helped sir. All killings get reported – freedom of the press and all that democratic stuff.'

'I know that but I'm getting a hammering from the Home Secretary every time there's a mention in the papers. It wouldn't be so bad if you'd got rid of Hakim in the first place. She's the one who killed Sir Michael and while she's alive there's always the danger that the allegations behind the Williams killing gains credence. If that happens the government could go down along with myself and anybody I can take with me. Do you understand Thomas?'

'Indeed I do sir.'

'Well you'd better act damn fast. You're not injured are you?'

'A few scratches and bruises but nothing to speak of.'

'Good where's your knife?'

'No problem. Took it with me.'

'Good. Now complete your mission and then go on holiday. Keep me informed.'

'Yes sir.'

Joshua put the phone down and summoned his PA.

'Hi Sam. Do you still want to press charges against Thomas?'

'Of course I do. What's the problem?'

'Well, he still hasn't completed his mission and I'm asking you to hold off until I give the all clear.'

'Okay but the longer I hold off, the weaker my claim, so I'm going to the police in any case.'

'There's no point. The police answer to me on these matters and I will tell them not to charge until I say so. It's best for all of us if you keep this little matter quiet for the time being Sam. I've already given you a pay increase. Remember that. To put it another way, if you go to the police, don't bother coming back here – your contract will be terminated.'

Samantha left the room slamming the door as she did so. She felt nothing was going to be done and the whole thing swept under the carpet. She'd been doing her own detective work since following Thomas to the tavern in Holborn. She'd kept an eye on him firstly, because he was no good, and secondly, because what she was finding out would be great material for her next novel! Now that he'd raped her she had even more on him and was going to use that to her best advantage. She decided to phone him and arrange a meeting.

The next day Nathan phoned Thomas:

'Congratulations Thomas. Othman is dead.'

'Nothing to do with me James.'

'Of course not. But there is a problem.'

'What's that?'

'I've just been summoned to the local police station. Something about an inquiry into my medical practices. You don't know anything about this do you old boy?'

'No, nothing. Perhaps Othman wrote a letter of complaint.'

'Did you see any letter...you would tell me Thomas wouldn't you.'

'Of course I would and no, I haven't seen anything.'

'Okay, I'll see what these clowns have to say but if it gets a bit heated can I rely on you guys to exert your authority?'

'Of course James – that's what old chums are for.'

'Thanks, I'll keep in touch.'

James Nathan made his way to Warren Street Station and was told to sit in the waiting room. It was a hot day for this time of year. The room was grubby, humid and claustrophobic – there were no windows. The chairs were all positioned along the four walls and had been constructed with a chrome finish apart from the seats which were covered with blue plastic vinyl - the type which made the bum sweaty! In the middle of the room was a coffee table with various police magazines strewn over the dirty surface. It was a place you did not want to be and nor did James Nathan whose posterior was becoming decidedly wet!

Inspector Francis entered the room and beckoned Nathan to follow him. They went down a number of corridors until they reached the interview rooms.

'I'm Inspector Nigel Francis of the Metropolitan Police and have been assigned as the investigating officer. You are Mr James Nathan?'

'That is correct officer, I'm sure we can sort this matter out straight away.'

'I hope so sir. But first I would like you to read this documentation.'

Francis handed Othman's letter and enclosures to Nathan.

'Take your time sir.'

Nathan read the papers and looked at Francis:

'So what?'

'Well do you accept the allegations?'

'Certainly not. It's all rubbish. I carried out tests, gave my diagnosis and applied the appropriate treatment. It's all down to my opinion based on the facts at the time. I happen to be one of the leading specialists in breast cancer treatment officer, surely you're not questioning my opinion?'

'Of course not sir – that's for others to investigate. I'm more interested in your relationship with Mr Maximilian Gustav and whether you have profited from alleged malpractice.'

'Certainly not.'

'So you deny the charges.'

'Of course I do. I need to phone my solicitor.'

'Certainly sir. In fact you can go now. Doubtless we and others will be in contact with you, so don't leave the country until this matter is resolved. Oh, and for your information, we have already contacted Mr Gustav who, like you, has denied everything.'

'There's nothing to deny. We're both totally innocent.'

'Fine sir, you may go.'

CHAPTER TWENTY-FIVE

Rania made her way to Highgate Cemetery looking decidedly worse for wear. She had a cut over her left eye which, although not deep, was certainly visible and her forehead was badly bruised. Her cheekbone had been broken and, again, a bruise was forming around the side of her face. Several people glanced at her as she passed them in the street. One kindly person stopped her and asked whether she needed any help. Rania declined but thought she'd better search for a chemist.

The rain pelted down as she entered the main gates of the cemetery. It was a gloomy day with no prospect of a reprieve in the weather. The chemist had been unhelpful and, apart from applying a plaster to her cut, advised her to see her GP as there was not much more he could do. It was at this point that Rania decided to buy an umbrella to keep dry and, because of its shape, to hide her face. Despite her injuries she still looked elegant; tall, slender, flowing black hair, smartly dressed and wearing sun glasses, she managed to portray the beautiful heroine in a Bond movie.

There was a small crowd surrounding a plot of land at the very back of the cemetery. She recognised some of the faces. Most of the mourners were from the museum as Angus had very few relatives. She stood behind the crowd for a few minutes and then made eye contact with some of the staff she recognised. They exchanged sympathetic smiles and then bowed their heads as an entourage carrying the coffin made its way towards the scene.

Without too much ceremony the coffin was lowered into the grave and people began throwing flowers into the pit before the diggers started their work. The vicar said a few words and Rania began to cry. The reality of the situation – a very good friend who'd saved her life - had died and here he was being buried. He had been kind to her and now he was gone. She would never see him again. It seemed the only men who'd cared for her were destined to suffer an early death. She cried for Rob, she cried for Angus but mostly she cried for herself because of the predicament she found herself. In fact she was inconsolable and after the prayers a couple of colleagues put their arms around her to comfort her. Their attempts, although prompted by genuine caring natures, and although graciously received, were futile and Rania, not wishing to ponder on the scene for another moment, made her exit running up the hill to the main gates. At this point she stopped to regain composure and to catch her breath. She hung on to the railings and sank down to the ground. She had nothing left and offered herself to Allah. And then she heard a kind voice:

'Are you Rania Hakim?'

Rania removed her glasses and looked up. She saw an elderly gentleman, probably not from the UK, head neatly shaven with a scar running down his face, and with a smile which revealed beautiful white teeth and which, for Rania, lit up an otherwise dark and gloomy world. She wiped the tears from her eyes and gazed into his face.

'Yes, I'm Rania Hakim. Who are you?'

'Mohammed Ishmail. We spoke this morning.'

'Oh yes. How did you know I was here?'

'You told me, don't you remember?'

'No, but I'm thankful you're here. I need someone to talk to.'

'Of course you do. Now let's get you to our place so you can meet Magda.'

Mohammed helped Rania to her feet and held her arm as they made their way towards the underground. From the other side of the road behind a great metal gate Thomas DeVelt watched them disappear over the hill.

⟞⟐⟝

The journey didn't take long and Rania soon found herself facing Magda with a cup of tea in her hand. The room was pleasantly decorated and, although they hadn't planned to stay long, Magda had applied her domestic skills to good effect. The table was covered with a tasteful tablecloth which she had bought in a local market; the sofa was adorned with luxurious cushions, again purchased locally, and on the wall was a framed photograph of her family. She had converted the rented accommodation into a home.

'How are you?' Rania asked. 'Othman told me about your treatment.'

'Much better now my dear. I've had my operation and the doctors say that it was very successful. I've completed my radiotherapy and they've said I can go home for my chemotherapy.'

'That's great news. When do you leave?'

'We haven't decided yet. Now that Othman's dead, everything has changed?'

'What do you mean?'

'Well, he was a very close friend and, as you may know, helped to pay for my treatment. We know that he liked you very much and went out of his way to protect you.'

'That's true.'

'We don't know all the background, of course, but whatever he did he had good reason. He was always keen on justice – doing the right thing – and his last wish was to expose the malpractice of Mr Nathan. I have a copy of his letter. Mohammed and I didn't wish to make a fuss but now that Othman is dead, the least we can do is pursue a claim in his honour – it's the right thing to do. I feel stronger now so I phoned the police and a nice gentleman asked me to meet with him at the police station tomorrow.'

'Where?'

'Warren Street.'

'Do you know who you're going to meet?'

'An Inspector Francis. He seemed very nice on the phone.'

'I'll come with you.'

'There's no need my dear.'

'I think there is. Let me tell you my story.'

Mohammed came in with some more tea and offered Rania some cake. He sat down with Magda and put his arm around her shoulders.

'Don't mind me. Tell us your story Rania.'

'Well, going back a year or so I found myself working for the United Nations in Baghdad. I was a clerk helping the scientists find evidence of weapons of mass destruction. No evidence was found as far as I was aware. Anyway, I met a man called Dr Rob Williams from the British government or MI5 or CIA or whatever they called it, and we got on really well. He was keen on archaeology so I took him to a nearby site. After that he went back to the UK and I got a job as a research assistant in the Cairo Museum. Everything changed from that point. I was followed home one night and got beaten up. The police gave me protection to begin with but then stopped because they didn't have enough resources. They had to give priority to other cases. All their investigations ceased. One of my colleagues was then killed by the same man, I think, who beat me up. Something was not right. Rob had been very vocal about there not being weapons of mass destruction and I think this got him into trouble. At the same time, because I was associated with him, I guessed they wanted to keep me quiet. My thinking was that if they, who ever 'they' were, wanted to hurt me, then they also wanted to hurt Rob. I therefore warned him. Next thing I knew he was on a plane to Cairo. We met and we fell in love. This was wrong of course as he was a married man, but we couldn't help ourselves. Anyway, we were warned that we were in danger. That's when I met Othman. He reckoned that I was being harassed in order to entice Rob over to Egypt and away from the UK. He thought the UK government or MI5 or the CIA had hired a contractor to frighten me and kill Rob. This was all theoretical of course, but this is what he believed. He organised a safe house for me and Rob but, unfortunately, this contractor tracked us down and, to cut a long story short, murdered Rob.'

'This sounds incredible' said Magda. 'Surely the UK was not behind this poor man's killing?'

'It's incredible but true. We shall never get to the bottom as to who was behind the killing, but let me continue. There's worse to come!'

'Mohammed, get some more tea. I think we may be here for some time.'

'No, I'll keep it short, although I wouldn't mind some more tea please. Where was I? Right, Othman was put in charge of the case and eventually caught the contractor who claimed that both the CIA and MI5 were behind the killing. He told Othman that he would 'spill the beans' if he were taken to court. The interesting thing is that before he was caught an attempt was made on his life by an MI5 operative.

Perhaps they knew he would disclose everything at some stage so they decided to bump him off. Unfortunately, the operative died in the attempt and the contractor escaped only to be arrested by Othman.'

'This is getting complicated. It's like one of those thrillers you see on television' said Mohammed.

'I know but just you wait. The operative had a photograph of the Head of MI5 and written on the back was a love note from him to her. They were obviously having an affair. Anyway, with an MI5 operative attempting to kill a contractor who then disclosed he was being paid by MI5 to murder Rob, it doesn't take a genius to realise that, in all probability, the Head of MI5 or, at least MI5, sanctioned the killing.'

'But I bet they deny it' said Magda.

'Of course they do. As it happened the contractor was shot dead before he went to court so justice was done as far as he was concerned. You may remember accommodating a Greek girl before shipping her down to Khartoum?'

'I remember. Her name was Helena. She was raped and assaulted by this contractor. That's why she killed him I suppose?' said Mohammed.

'That's right. A nice girl. Hope she's okay now. Othman gave me the photograph of the Head of MI5.'

'Why?'

'Good question. Either because he had in mind that I would exact revenge on my lover's killer or I would deal with matters some other way to bring the man or organisation or both to justice.'

'Crafty but at the same time naive' said Mohammed. 'You'd be fighting the establishment. People would just simply deny it.'

'I know, that's why I killed him.'

'What?'

'Yes, it was the only way to achieve justice. It was an honour killing.'

'I don't think the English courts would look at it like that, but I understand your feelings' said Magda.

'Anyway, I got a job in the British Museum and the case against me was dropped. I had two alibis and no one could identify me because I was covered from head to foot like a good Muslim. And then an Inspector Nigel Francis confronted me threatening to resurrect the case through the media – unless I paid him money.'

'Blackmail?'

'Exactly. More worrying was that he was going to cite Othman as an accomplice as he'd handed me the photo.'

'See what I mean by naivety?' said Mohammed.

'I know. Othman went to see him as they were old buddies at university. He was hoping that if he told Francis the whole story, he would drop the case. Unfortunately, according to Othman, his old mate had changed and he had no intention of dropping the case.'

'So what did Othman do?'

'Refused to pay him anything. There then followed a press release saying that the police were applying to the CPS for a resurrection of the case against me.'

'And has the case been resurrected?'

'Not yet. Othman believed there wouldn't be a resurrection as my evidence would refer to the Rob Williams case which would frighten the government. He believed they wanted to let 'sleeping dogs lie'. The last thing they wanted was to have a public debate on Rob's case.'

'What happened next?'

'I and a colleague were attacked on our way to my home in Barnes. He got killed trying to protect me, hence the funeral this morning. Then yesterday I believe the same man killed Othman.'

'Who is this man?'

'Well, Othman believed that MI5 were involved again. The government knew that I killed the Head of MI5 but did not want a resurrection of the Rob Williams case. On the other hand, justice had to be administered, that is, the murderer had to be caught and dealt with. Neither the police or the government wanted to get involved so assigned this task to MI5. Their methods are plain for all to see – simply murder the suspects and anybody associated with them.'

'And Inspector Francis? Is he the same Francis we're seeing tomorrow?'

'I expect so. He can't be trusted. He and his bosses are probably told what to do by MI5. That's why I want to come with you tomorrow. He may say he's going to take up your case but may not if he's being pressurised. After all, you're questioning the ethics of the medical fraternity and, in cases like these, they all stick together and close ranks.'

'There must be someone in the government who's beyond all reproach.'

'Well, the letter and enclosures have been sent to a lot of people. Let's just hope that the BMA or the Health Secretary are beyond reproach and are prepared to stand up and be counted.'

'What about you Rania?' said Mohammed. 'You're in grave danger. If you're right about all this you're on top of their list?'

'I know, but I don't care anymore. I've seen too many deaths. People that I've loved have died for me. I'm hoping I'll meet them soon in a place which is free from hate.'

'God willing you will, but not just yet. You have your whole life to lead. The best thing you can do is get the next flight to Cairo.'

'Thanks Magda. But that's not the answer. They have contacts in Cairo. I won't be safe anywhere. I'm going to stand my ground here in honour of Othman. I'm going to help you with your claim and get justice for him. That's the least I can do. If I die in the process, then so be it.'

'You my dear have courage' said Magda. 'I cannot condone what you've done but you have been true to yourself and loyal to others. May Allah judge you kindly.'

CHAPTER TWENTY-SIX

Samantha arranged to meet Thomas in the *Princess Louise* pub in Holborn at 7.00 pm. She arrived at 7.15 pm and saw him drinking a beer in a corner at the back of the pub. She switched on her recording device as she made her way towards him. The pub was crowded with office workers who'd finished their day's work and needed some refreshment before venturing home to face irritated partners who were not part of the office set. Teams in London tended to work hard but played harder, and after seven hours of political manoeuvring (otherwise known as' bitching'), there was nothing like a further onslaught on unpopular colleagues in the pub away from those whose backs were likely to be stabbed.

Samantha was well accustomed to this ritual and took every opportunity to 'bitch' behind people's backs although, in MI5, she had to know where and when to draw the line. Her antics, in terms of the use of her body, were well known although never spoken of as few operatives wanted to admit they'd paid for her services. However, after a couple of drinks in the pub, even Samantha was surprised at the lack of re-straint demonstrated by some of the younger mem-bers who became quite vocal in expressing their desperation for sex with the Head's PA. Samantha took all this in her stride and let their ranting and ravings flow over her as she always had 'bigger fish to fry'.

'Hi Sam. Sit down. Look I'm terribly sorry for what happened. I was pissed and stupid. You know I'm not normally like that.'

'Thomas, did you rape me or not?'

'I can't quite remember.'

'Then why are you saying sorry?'

'Because I am. I know I behaved badly.'

'Do you remember me saying no and trying to get away from you?'

'Well sort of, but I thought you really wanted it.'

'But I said no and no means no. You forced your-self on to me.'

'I'm sorry, it will never happen again.'

'Do you remember hitting me as I tried to leave?'

'I don't remember hurting you in any way.'

'Bullshit, you smacked me around the mouth and pushed me against the door.'

'I know, I know, but I didn't hurt you. It was only a tap, you weren't seriously hurt.'

'That's not the point. You raped and assaulted me.'

'You're going over the top now Sam. Can't we make up and have a nice drink together?'

'Okay but no more violent performances. I'll give you one more chance.'

'That's my girl. Now what will it be?'

'Double vodka and lemonade and another one after that.'

The two of them spent the next hour drinking and joking about some of the eccentric staff in MI5. Samantha was spent by 9.00 pm and Thomas offered to accompany her home. They got the bus to Bayswater and Thomas escorted her to her apartment. She invited him in and told him to make himself a drink. She was shattered. She left her handbag on the sofa and threw her jacket on the armchair. After a drunken apology she disappeared into the bedroom.

Thomas made himself a cup of coffee and looked round the room. It was basic, functional and bland.

The walls were painted light brown and all the furniture was made out of tubular metal with a chrome finish. There were no pictures on the wall apart from a photo of Sam in her underwear and the only plant in the room was artificial.

He finished his coffee and went into the kitchen. Again, basic and functional. He noticed a bottle of whisky on the table, unscrewed the cap and took a gulp straight from the bottle. He went back to the lounge with bottle in hand and sat on the sofa. He took another gulp. He closed his eyes and thought about Rania Hakim. He knew he had to act fast but couldn't afford to make any more mistakes. He thought about Sam. Yes, he remembered raping and assaulting her, but he wasn't going to admit it. It was her word against his. Anyway, she deserved it. She was no more than a whore; a slag; a tart – he couldn't care less if she ended up dead. He became annoyed and agitated. He noticed the handbag and checked the bedroom door to make sure there was no movement. He went up to the door and listened. Samantha was snoring like a pig. Good, he thought to himself and went back to the sofa. He opened the handbag and rummaged round the contents. Usual things – lipstick, tissues, polo mints, brushes, condoms, photographs, and two small recording devices.

He had another gulp of the whisky and played the tapes. Bitch, he mumbled to himself, she's going to stitch him up. She's probably been told to wait until his mission is over. Bitch he said in a louder tone, bitch, bitch, bitch. He had another gulp and got up to go to the loo, leaving the devices on the sofa. He staggered across the floor and found it difficult to open the door. He eventually got in and slumped round the toilet seat in a drunken stupor. He dozed off but was woken up by movement in the flat.

'What's the matter with you?' Samantha asked. She had a towel rapped round her body which made her backside look even bigger than Blackpool. 'Are you pissed again?'

'You bitch Sam, you taped our conversation on two occasions.'

'You've gone through my handbag. Why did you do that?'

'It was there on the sofa. I was intrigued.'

'Well, you shouldn't have done. Anyway, so what if I did. You're going down on this one Thomas and nothing's going to stop me from going to the police. In fact, I've already been'.

'They'll never believe you. It's you word against mine.'

'We both know the truth. I'll make them believe me.'

'With your reputation, you haven't got a chance.'

'We'll see about that.' Samantha rushed to the sofa and grabbed the tapes. Thomas sprung from the toilet seat and grabbed the towel which left Samantha completely naked. He rubbed himself against her back while squeezing her breasts with both hands.'

'Get off' she screamed and elbowed him in the stomach. He doubled up and she made for the door. She managed to get her coat on and unlock the door, but Thomas, quickly recovering, flew at her with the whisky bottle in his hand.

'Don't 'she screamed, but it was too late. Thomas smashed the bottle over her head causing her skull to crack. She fell to the floor and, in a fit of uncontrollable rage, he continued to beat her with what was now a broken bottle.

'You bitch, you bitch' he cried. 'You whoring slag. You deserve this.'

By this time there was blood oozing from several head wounds and, indeed, from deep cuts in her back. The door was splattered with blood along with the adjoining wall and carpets. Thomas's hand and the bottle he held were also reddened along with his trousers and shirt. He grabbed his jacket and stumbled to the front door falling over Samantha's body in the process. He rushed down the stairs into the gardens of the apartment block where he took refuge behind a large privet hedge. His senses told him to stay where he was until the streets were quiet which meant he would have to wait for at least another three hours. This he did and when it was quiet he made his escape by foot, running northwards and looking out for a suitable taxi cab service – one that looked seedy, dirty and illegal. On his journey he discarded the bottle in a dustbin and checked that his jacket was buttoned up to cover the blood stains on his shirt. He washed his hands and face in a puddle and combed his hair using the reflection in a shop window. He got home by 4.00 am, had a shower and washed his clothes.

Next morning he phoned Joshua and let him know what happened.

'You what?' Joshua screamed.

'I lost it sir. She was going to the police with a recording of our conversation. I had no choice.'

'Of course you had choices you idiot. You're a liability Thomas. I'll try to give you cover but I can't hold off the Met forever.'

'You could say it was in the line of duty sir. She knew too much and had to go.'

'I could say that, but it would be a lie. There's only so much cover up I can get away with.'

'Please do your best sir. Meanwhile I'll sort out Hakim and then disappear.'

'I wish you would. I better phone the Deputy Chief Constable and see what he can do. From now on Thomas, you're on your own. You'll stay on the payroll for the time being but once you've finished the job, you'll have to go. I'll make sure you get a decent bonus but only after, I repeat after, you've done the business.'

'Thank you sir.'

Joshua hung up and phoned Richard Scott, Deputy Chief Constable. A young lady answered and told him that he had better speak to the Chief Constable, Peter Falkner. Falkner had been Chief for about four years and many believed he was on his way out. He hadn't met his crime figures and had made himself a bit of a nuisance with government ministers. A quiet man who hadn't been through university but had proved himself in many ways – including his handling of politicians. That's probably why they didn't like him.

'Where's Richard, Peter?'

'Good morning Josh and how are you?'

'Yes, good morning, but I need to speak to Richard.'

'Why might I ask?'

'Oh just a matter that I know he can help me with.'

'And what would that be?'

'Look Peter I'm in a hurry. Richard knows the background and, quite frankly, I haven't got time to go through the whole thing with you.'

'Well Josh you're going to have to because Richard has been suspended from duty?'

'What?'

'You heard.'

'But why?.'

'Shall we just say that he was failing to keep me in the loop on too many occasions. HR have labelled it insubordination but I rather like the phrase 'complicit in a cover up' – does that mean anything to you Josh, me old mate?'

'Don't know what you're talking about Peter.'

'Well, it doesn't matter, I'm in charge now. I'm not on my way out as Richard thought and I'm ready to do business with the honourable MI5. Now fill me in. I assume you're phoning me because a crime has been committed and you want me to cover it up?'

'Of course not.'

'Well then, what do you want, but make it fast cos I've got a meeting with the PM in 15 minutes.'

Joshua realised he'd have to disclose Samantha's murder. He decided to keep quiet about Thomas and play for time until he'd done the business. He was taking a risk, of course, perverting the course of justice and all that, but he was the Head of MI5 responsible for national security and, indeed, had been instructed by the Home Secretary himself to deal with the Rania Hakim situation – after all she had killed his predecessor and, therefore, posed a threat to Blighty – who else might she murder? These thoughts quickly ran through his head as he anticipated his next move with the Chief Constable.

'What I was going to tell Richard was that it has come to our attention that a crime has been committed in Bayswater. We found out about it a few minutes ago from an anonymous caller. We're told that the victim is one Samantha Wilson, my PA. You better get your lads down there pronto.'

'Thanks for the tip off Josh. I'll get on to it straight away.'

⊷ ⊶

Inspector Nigel Francis got a call from the Chief Constable and was summoned to his office. He was unaware that the Deputy Chief Constable had been suspended and assumed Richard would be at the meeting. He phoned Mohammed Ishmail, postponed the meeting and quickly made his way to Scotland Yard.

'Ah Nigel, take a seat.'

'Where's Richard sir?'

'He's been suspended. He was getting a bit too big for his boots. I can't say more than that. Look Nigel, we haven't got long. I've read your personal file and, I have to say, you're good cop.'

'Thank you sir.'

'But, there's been a few instances recently where I've questioned whether you really are a good cop.'

'Sir, I can expl...'

'Don't speak Inspector, I want to get this off my chest once and for all. I've dealt with Richard and now I'm going to deal with you. I've spoken to the Home secretary so I know what's been going on. You blackmailed both Rania Hakim and Inspector Othman, threatening to use the press to resurrect the case against her. That was wrong and had I known about your antics, I would have fired you. I would have also let you hung out to dry in the courts. Richard, or should I say Dickie, kept me out of the loop thinking I was going under. That was a big mistake and he will suffer the consequences. Let's get this straight; on matters of crime in this country we don't report or pander to MI5. We do our jobs fairly and independently. Richard told me, under 'torture' I might add, that the Head of MI5 had told him not repeat not to investigate an allegation of rape and assault until he gave permission. That was wrong, wrong, wrong. MI5 have no jurisdiction over us in these matters. Richard was out of order and should have told MI5 to get stuffed. Rape is a crime and we investigate crimes immediately – we don't wait for MI5 to tell us when to start investigations.' There was a pause. 'Are you getting this Inspector?'

'Yes sir.'

'Good. You'd better. From now on you take orders from me, not anyone else. No, I'm not promoting you to Deputy Chief – you won't be ready for a long time, but I am going to give you a chance to redeem yourself. You must understand though – no more corruption, no more bribery, no more blackmailing – any further mishaps of this nature and you'll be out. Consider this to be your final warning even though according to HR it probably isn't. But take it from me it is.'

'Got it?'

'Yes sir.'

'Well it so happens that this person who was raped was the PA to the Head of MI5. I say was because the said Samantha Wilson was murdered yesterday. I want you to get your arse down to Bayswater and head up the investigation.'

'Thank you sir. I'll get on to it straight away.'

'Oh and Nigel. One last thing. When Samantha was raped she reported the crime to the police citing a Mr Thomas DeVelt as the perpetrator. Again, under 'torture', Dickie admitted he was aware of this. Thomas DeVelt is a senior operative working for MI5. There may be a connection between the rape and the murder, I don't know. Remember Inspector – fair play from now on – or else.'

'Right sir.'

CHAPTER TWENTY-SEVEN

Nigel found the apartment block in Bayswater and noticed two ambulances and three police cars parked in a nearside road. He peered into the backs of the ambulances to make sure there were no occupants. He then dashed up the stairs and found the whole of the first floor cordoned off with two police officers guarding the front door. He showed them his pass and stepped into the room where the murder had been committed. He assumed it was murder as he could tell from observing the wound that the blow on Samantha's head could not have been self- inflicted, nor could it have been an accident. The forensics were busying themselves with all sorts of measurements, samplings and assessments while the three ambulance men looked on from the corner of the room. There were three other policemen standing together, milling around by the kitchen door.

'Who got here first?' he asked them.

'I did sir' said the youngest looking policeman.

'What time?'

'About 10.00 this morning. We got a call from a neighbour who lives downstairs. She said she heard a lot of shouting and screaming last night. Didn't think much of it but when she investigated this morning, noticed a bit of blood on the landing floor. That's when she called us.'

'Where is she now?'

'Downstairs sir in flat one.'

'Okay, I'll go down to see her in a minute.' Nigel turned to the forensics team. 'Who's in charge guys?'

'I suppose I am' said a young lady who was busy counting the cuts on Samantha's back.'

'Time of death?'

'Can't be sure at this stage Inspector, my guess is that this lady died around 10.30 to 10.45 pm last night.'

'How did she die.'

'Loss of blood to the head and back.'

'How was it done?'

'Again, can't be sure but it seems like it could have been a bottle. Someone must have smashed her on the head. The bottle broke on impact and the attacker must have used the jagged edge to make the cuts on her back. It looks like a frenzied attack.'

'Nice. Have we got the bottle?'

'No, but we've got samples of glass. We've got finger prints everywhere so it shouldn't be difficult to make an identification.'

Nigel turned to the policemen and asked them whether they had looked outside for any evidence.

'Yes sir but we can't find anything obvious. The forensics are taking samples of everything including the doors and front gate.'

'Okay. I'm going to pop downstairs to see the neighbour. Let me know if you find anything else.'

Nigel took the stairs to the ground floor and knocked on flat one's door. An elderly lady answered. She was wearing a dressing gown and looked decidedly shocked.

'Hello, I'm Inspector Francis. Can I have a word?'

'Yes, come in. I'm a bit fragile at the moment but this nice lady has been keeping me company.' She pointed to a policewoman sitting on the sofa.

'Do you want a cup of tea Inspector?'

'No thanks. Can I take your name?'

'Oh it's Matilda. Matilda Wilkins. That's my married name. My maiden name is Stott but I much prefer Wilkins. I was so happy when I got married because I'd always hated the name Stott.'

'Why's that Mrs Wilkins?'

'Oh, it's such an ugly sounding name. I much prefer Wilkins. My husband died five years ago and I thank God every night that he left me with such a perfect surname. I couldn't spend the rest of my life with a name like Stott. That's why I married Henry – he had such a lovely name.'

Nigel exchanged glances with the policewoman who'd obviously concluded, the same as he; that Mrs Wilkins may not be of sound mind.

'Can you tell me what happened last night Mrs Stott, I mean Mrs. Wilkins?'

'Well I watched my favourite programmes, made myself a cup of tea and went to bed. I go through that routine every night.'

'Didn't you hear noises from upstairs?'

'What Samantha's flat? Let me think...yes, now you mention it there was some shouting.'

'What did you do?'

'Do?...I didn't do anything?'

'Why not?'

'Well Samantha is a lovely girl but she often screams and shouts. I suppose that's what all young people do nowadays – scream and shout. Didn't the Beatles sing that song about screaming and shouting?'

'No, that was 'Twist and Shout' Mrs Wilkins' said the policewoman.'

'Well, whatever, Sam has a lot of boyfriends and they're always making noises. Brings back happy memories when Henry and I had such fun. You can't blame the youngsters Inspector – they've got to have their play time.'

'So you went to bed, heard noises from upstairs but didn't think anything about it because such noises were not unusual?'

'That's right.'

'What did you do when you woke up this morning?'

'Well, I did what I normally do.'

'What's that?' asked the policewoman.

'I took up a small bottle of semi skimmed milk for Sam.' Her face changed from happy to sad. Her jaw dropped and she looked scared. She started to cry. 'When I reached her door I put the milk on the floor and noticed the carpet was stained red. It was everywhere. I hadn't noticed it before. At first I thought it was the pattern of the carpet but then I thought it can't be as there's no red stain around my front door. I then remembered my poor old Henry when he cut his hand. There was blood all over the carpet. It looked exactly like the stain I saw around Sam's door. I thought this can't be right. I shouted out for Henry but then I thought what a silly old fool I was because he'd been dead for a long time. I didn't know what to do so I phoned my friend, Freda. She told me to phone the police which I did. Then the door rang and this nice police officer suggested we had a cup of tea. Then you came in and I offered you a cup of tea. Is everything alright Inspector? Where's Sam? Has she gone to work? What's happened?'

'Thanks Mrs Wilkins, your friend Sam has had a nasty accident. I'm afraid she's dead.'

There was a pause. Mrs Wilkins looked very worried and confused.

'No, that can't be right. She often screamed but she was never in any trouble. I always saw her the next day,'

'Well, I'm sorry Mrs Wilkins, but you were right to call the police. Thank you very much. Do you have any friends or relatives?'

'Only Freda.'

'Do you want to see her?'

'I suppose so – what a to-do – what will Freda say? I don't want to frighten her.'

'Officer, I must go now. Could you look after Mrs Wilkins until Freda arrives'. He turned to Mrs Wilkins –' Why don't you phone her and invite her round for tea.'

Her expression changed. She stopped sobbing and became very calm.

'Oh officer, I wish I could. Poor old Freda passed away this time last year...or was it the year before. I don't know. My memory seems to be fading fast. Good bye Inspector, I hope you can clear up that mess upstairs. I don't think I've the strength. Any way I've run out of bleach. I think I'll go to bed now if you don't mind.'

Nigel left Mrs Wilkins in the care of the police-woman and went back up stairs. This time he noticed the blood by the front door – in fact, he noticed even more blood in the front room as Samantha's body had been transferred via plastic bag to the ambulance on her journey to the morgue.

He told the policemen to wait until the forensic team had finished and then arrange for a clear up. He was told by forensics that it would take another week to complete their investigations and a further week to finalise autopsy results. In the meantime he would phone Mohammed Ishmail to arrange a meeting.

The Times ran the following story:

PA TO HEAD OF MI5 FOUND BRUTALLY MURDERED

A Miss Samantha Wilson was found dead on 21st September 2004 at her Bayswater apartment. Initial reports show that she was probably killed around 10.30 the previous night. Miss Wilson was the personal assistant to Mr Joshua Wilson-Smith, Head of MI5, and had been working for this organisation for about five years.

It is alleged that Miss Wilson was bludgeoned with a bottle with such force that it cracked her skull. This, together with serious lacerations to the back, indicates that she died from these injuries. A post mortem will be arranged in due course. The police as yet have no idea who the murderer could be, although they are optimistic an identification will be made as finger prints were left all over the apartment and on Miss Wilson's body.

Mr Wilson-Smith stated: 'I am shocked by this terrible news. Sam was a loyal and efficient member of staff and I am at a total loss as to why this has happened and who has committed such a terrible crime. My condolences go out to her friends and family.'

Inspector Francis of the Metropolitan Police states: 'This is a particularly nasty crime with no obvious motive or suspect. Forensics are doing a great job in analysing the evidence found at the scene and I am optimistic that a positive identification will be made very soon.'

Investigations continue.

CHAPTER
TWENTY-EIGHT

The Home Secretary read this article twice and then phoned Joshua telling him to get over to his office straight away. While he waited he read the article a third time and requested coffee from his secretary. He advised her that the Head of MI5 was about to make a visit and that he shouldn't be disturbed. He told her he wanted complete privacy and asked her to have an early lunch.

When Joshua arrived he found the Home Secretary sitting on his secretary's desk.

'Ah Joshua, come into my office. Have you seen the headlines?'

'Yes sir.'

'Do you know anything about this Josh because if you do you'd better tell me everything.'

Joshua realised he had to make a full disclosure.

'It was Thomas DeVelt sir. He phoned me and confessed the other night.'

'Thomas DeVelt, your operative?'

'Yes sir.'

'I'm shocked.' There was a pause while the Home Secretary looked out of his window with a concerned look on his face.

'But why?'

'Long story sir. Basically, he'd previously raped her. She'd taped everything and went to the police. I told the Deputy Chief Constable to hold off until DeVelt had completed his mission.'

'Which was what?'

'To deal with Ms Rania Hakim.'

'You mean kill her?'

'Yes sir, as we agreed.'

'I didn't agree to anything like that Josh. When I say deal with the matter, that doesn't necessarily mean murder. That sort of stuff is up to you and has nothing to do with the government.'

'I know sir. But evidently she'd taped various conversations she'd had with DeVelt and, on finding the recordings, he went berserk and killed her. I told the police about the murder but didn't tell them it was DeVelt.'

'Why not.'

'Again I wanted him to finish the job. Don't forget sir, Hakim had killed Sir Michael Wilkinson and the government didn't want the Rob Williams case to hit the headlines again. That's why we agreed not to resurrect the case against her but to remove her in some other way.'

'Am I right in saying that on this dubious journey both Professor Lear and Inspector Othman were killed?'

'Yes sir.'

'By DeVelt?'

'Yes sir.'

'I see, now, in a fit of rage he's killed yet another innocent victim and is about to kill a fourth?'

'Yes sir, although Inspector Othman was not entirely innocent and Rania Hakim certainly isn't.'

'I don't need to tell you Josh that this is getting far too messy. You and your incompetent operative have gone too far and...'

'But sir, this was all agreed. We were doing this for national security reasons. It was a shame that the Professor and Ms Wilson got in the way, but that's the way it is.'

'You're right to a degree. Unfortunately the whole thing has been bungled which, as far as I'm concerned, has blurred any arguments for preserving national security. You will have to tell the Chief Constable of course and explain to him why you have withheld evidence. Perverting the course of justice springs to mind. You can use the national security argument but I don't think that'll wash with him. He seems to have become more and more assertive recently. And another thing, the government, and more importantly myself, know nothing about the background to these murders – do you understand Josh? We never sanctioned any killings; that was down to you and no one else.'

'I know sir, but we were just doing the job we were paid to do. We are no more than an agency doing your dirty work.'

'You and I are going to fall out very soon. I repeat, we have never sanctioned any killings. We just wanted matters resolved in the interests of national security. If MI5 interpret that as meaning bumping off anybody who gets in the way, then that's down to MI5 and no one else. Have you got that Josh?'

'Indeed I have sir.'

'Right from now on, I don't want to hear from you about this matter again. The police will have to handle it from this point. You don't have the jurisdiction to halt their enquiries and you certainly don't have the right to withhold evidence from them. That's the official line from now. Put a lid on this whole thing and your career might be saved. Any more cock ups – which could be anything from another murder to an article in the newspapers, means the end for you. I hope I make myself clear.'

'You certainly do sir. May I go now?'

Joshua got back to his office and rang Thomas. He told him that the government knew everything about the rape and killings and were not playing ball. Thomas was indignant and reminded him that he'd promised to hold off the police. Josh told him he couldn't do that any longer:

'You've gone rogue Thomas and now you need to disappear'.

'But my mission is incomplete.'

'It's finished now Thomas. I don't want to hear from you again. You're on your own. I'm removing you from the payroll.'

'On what grounds?'

'I think the murder of two innocent victims, bringing the name of the service into disrepute resulting in an irretrievable breakdown of trust and confidence, is enough to be going on with.'

'You've got to be joking, these murders were all part of the job.'

'Nonsense, I want nothing more to do with you. Your P45 will be in the post.'

'Well, you know I'll blab and bring you and everybody down.'

'That's your choice, now disappear, you're fired.'

CHAPTER TWENTY-NINE

Mohammed, Magda and Rania waited in the reception of the police station. Mohammed nervously held Othman's letter and pondered on how things had turned out. His dear and brave friend had died – brutally murdered by an unidentifiable assassin. His remains had been flown back to his family in Khartoum and the funeral ceremonies had been arranged. He'd died a hero, there was no doubt, and he would always be remembered. A good friend, a good policeman, a good human being – Mohammed wanted to take revenge on his killer, but didn't know where to start. He took comfort in the fact that he and his wife would be pursuing their claim against

Mr Nathan. Othman would have wanted this because he was a man of justice. Who knows, this man Francis might help them track down Othman's killer, especially as he was an old friend. His thoughts were interrupted by the opening of a door on the opposite side of the room. Inspector Nigel Francis rushed through to meet them and asked them to wait another five minutes. He looked at Rania and asked whether he could see her first. She agreed and followed him to a small interviewing room behind the reception area.

'Please sit down Rania. Look before we get going on this Nathan case, I just wanted to say sorry about my pathetic blackmail attempts. It was wrong and I guess I got too big for my boots. I've confessed and they're giving me another chance to make good. I intend to make good. I've been a fool. I'm sorry.'

'Well Inspector, I don't trust you and I'm surprised you're still a policeman. You've got to do a lot of making up before any kind of trust is restored.'

'I know that. But I also know that you killed Sir Michael Wilkinson. Othman told me everything'.

There was a long pause.

'I let him down, I know that, and now he's dead. I want to make things right. He obviously suspected Nathan of malpractice and, knowing Othman, he was probably right. The challenge will be to establish enough evidence to prove the case, made more difficult, of course, by the medical brotherhood. Nevertheless, I'll give it a go depending on what Magda can tell me. And then there's the matter of Othman's death. The police were told to drop their CPS application to resurrect the case against yourself, and simply walk away. We were invited to a meeting convened by the PM and Home Secretary. The Head of MI5 and an operative called Thomas DeVelt were also present. Anyway, after they told us to drop the case, we were asked to leave the room and let the government handle the situation. I suspect the Home Secretary told MI5 to sort it out and Thomas DeVelt was used as the hatchet man. Only a guess mind you but this guy is a rapist and, I suspect, a murderer, and it wouldn't surprise me one bit if he was Othman's killer.'

'I'm fed up with the whole thing Inspector. Three men have died for me – men who I was deeply fond of – and I don't think I can go on.'

'Don't talk like that Rania. You are young and, more to the point, alive. Let's sort out this Nathan character and then bring Othman's murderer to justice. You can then start afresh.'

'But I killed a man.'

'Yes, but you had your reasons and there's nothing more you can do about it.'

'Easy for you to say.'

'I know, but I've got my demons as well and behaved terribly towards you and Othman. I can't do much about that now, apart from apologise. We both have to move on, despite the past.'

'I guess so. Okay I'll give you a chance. Shall I call in Mohammed and Magda?'

'Please ... and Rania, thank you. I won't let you down from now on.'

Mohammed and Magda shuffled into the interview room and sat down opposite Nigel. Rania explained to them that they could trust him and that they must tell him everything they knew about Gustav and Nathan.

'Okay Magda, please start from the beginning' asked Nigel.

'Well. I got diagnosed with stage one breast cancer but couldn't have the operation because of the waiting list. Othman kindly offered to pay for my treatment and so I visited Mr Gustav who had a private practice. He told me that my cancer was advanced and unusual and that my best chance of survival was to go to England to get more specialised treatment. When I arrived in the UK Mr Nathan gave me some tests and told me there was blood in my urine. The records showed this was not the case. He then put me on chemotherapy for advanced cancer treatment. This was very toxic and made me feel dreadful. Othman managed to get the papers which proved I had early stage cancer and showed the difference between standard and advance treatment costs. This was all shown to Mr Nathan who simply denied the charges. That's it really. I then transferred to the Royal Marsden and had my operation. They confirmed stage one cancer. I feel fine now although I will have to complete my chemotherapy sessions in Cairo.'

'I'm pleased to hear that you're okay Magda' said Nigel. 'I have all the papers you mentioned and I have spoken to Mr Nathan. He denies everything of course. I agree with Othman, this entire thing looks very suspicious, but I don't know whether we can prove whether any criminal activity has taken place.'

'Why not?' asked Rania.

'Well, even if we could demonstrate that charges were made to the beneficiary and associated payments made to their personal accounts, what would this prove? They are both distinguished physicians operating in both private and public sectors. They could argue that it was their opinion (albeit proved wrong) that Magda suffered from advanced cancer and that the appropriate treatment was administered. As private practitioners they charged what they said they were going to charge, having agreed the costs with you, and pocketed the payments. I don't think we can prove any criminal activity from this perspective on the evidence we have to date. However, I believe there was malpractice. It's clear that you had stage one cancer so there was no need to apply advanced chemotherapy. I see that. But I'm not a medical professional and need an objective medical input.'

'So what do we do now?' asked Mohammed.

'Leave it with me. Assuming you haven't heard from the Health Secretary or any of the other people copied in on the correspondence, I'm going to have a little word with my newspaper friend. I'm going to stick my neck out and get this thing publicised – that's the least I can do. I'll also have a word with my boss who can get hold of the Health Secretary quicker than I can – he can get the wheels in motion.' The following week the headlines in *The Sun* read:

SUDANESE CANCER SUFFERER EXPLOITED BY THE MEDICAL MAFIA

A Sudanese woman with stage one breast cancer was told she had advanced cancer and subjected to vile toxic drugs for no reason. She was told by Mr James Nathan, a prominent cancer specialist, that her tests showed blood in the urine and stools when, in fact, this proved to be untrue. He then went on to administer highly expensive chemotherapy, normally used for advanced cancers, which, some believe, was to make money for himself and his accomplice in Cairo. Mr Nathan denied all charges. The woman was successfully treated at the Royal Marsden for early stage cancer - thus proving that the advanced treatment was unnecessary. The Health Secretary has ordered a full enquiry and states 'If these allegations prove to be true then the credibility of those involved will be damaged beyond all repair.' Meanwhile Mr Nathan has been instructed not to practice by the Department of Health and has been suspended from the NHS. He declined to make a statement. Investigations continue.

Following this announcement the Ishmails were flooded with calls from 'no win no fee' solicitors but declined the very generous offers made to them. They felt justice was taking its course and that nothing more could be done. They were not interested in compensation. They just wanted to go home.

⇒⊹ ⊹⇐

Thomas DeVelt got a call from James Nathan.

'Look where I've ended up Thomas. My career is in tatters. I thought you were going to sort it?'

'Sorry James but I did get rid of Othman for you. Unfortunately I've lost favour with the Head of MI5 so can't pull any more strings.'

'No but you can get rid of that damned Sudanese woman. I'll pay you of course.'

'Why do you want to get rid of her? You stitched her up?'

'I deny that. I'll argue that she's done all this to make some money. I'll argue that she had it in for me right from the very beginning. I'll say she wants her day in court and won't stop at anything to bring me down. I could have cured her without any damn operation Thomas, that's the point. If she'd just given me a chance, I could've explained.'

'Well you've still got a chance. Go to the press and give your side of the story.'

'Too late for that now, I'll take my chances at the Court of Enquiry. I'll get some of my medical mates from uni involved. But Thomas, I want her out of the way. I'll pay you. No one shows me up in public.'

'No James, that would be a step too far. I'm already in it up to my neck. I've been sacked.'

'Then earn yourself a bit of money. I'll pay you a year's wages.'

'That wouldn't be enough.'

'Okay two years wages.'

'Make it three and I'll think about it'

'How much would that be?'

'One hundred and sixty thousand, although I'd want half up front.'

'It's a deal.'

'Good although I won't move until the money is deposited in my account.'

'I'll get it in there by tomorrow.'

'Good, ta ta for now.'

With that kind of money he could make a new start in France or even Germany. However, he had one last job to complete – whether under the auspices of MI5 or not – he needed to fulfil his mission before Rania Hakim escaped to Cairo. He had absolutely no intention of killing Magda Ishmail. He'd just take half the money and disappear. His old chum Nathan would have to take his chances in court.

CHAPTER THIRTY

Rania was down. It was as if everything had caught up with her and the realisation of it all weighed heavily on her mind. She'd lost her job at the museum through redundancy although, she suspected, this was not the real reason – several of her work colleagues had mentioned the unwanted publicity whilst others mentioned her sickness. She'd been away from work since the death of the professor and the Greek Exhibition had been closed. In any event, none of this mattered now. Too much had happened and despite all that Nigel Francis had said, she saw no light at the end of the tunnel – only blackness. She was seriously depressed.

The Ishmails had accommodated her for the last few days and were becoming increasingly worried about her health. Eventually they had got her to see a doctor who diagnosed post- traumatic stress disorder and prescribed medication. Rania explained that she was not sleeping or eating and saw little point in going on. The doctor explained why she might be feeling like this and that made things better. She concluded in her own mind that she wasn't suicidal and decided to give the drugs a chance.

Her symptoms were worse first thing in the morning when she could hardly get out of bed. However, after a couple of hours she felt better and was able to force herself to undertake mundane things like showering, dressing and making a cup of tea. The Ishmails had kindly given up their bedroom to allow Rania her privacy while they could get on with their lives in the rest of the apartment. They didn't want to leave the UK until Rania was fit to travel. At that moment, she was far from fit and spent many hours just gazing out the window. Her mind focussed on two things – the death of her closest friends and the assassination of Sir Michael Wilkinson. Up to now, she had been able to divorce herself from these events, probably because the adrenaline in her body had diverted her attention, allowing her to concentrate on other things. That didn't matter now as the significance of what had happened weighed very heavily on her mind – and was causing her to be ill. After all, she did kill Sir Michael – there was no getting away from it, and, whether it was right or wrong, it was premeditated murder. The thought of hell gave her sleepless nights.

The Ishmails tried their best to support her. They took her out for long walks, made her nice meals and encouraged her to talk about her predicament, but nothing seemed to work and poor Rania went into further decline. The drugs were making her feel worse and when she went back to her doctor, she said that it could take another three weeks before the medication kicked in. This made Rania feel even worse because she didn't know whether she could bear the pain for another three weeks.

One morning after a good night's sleep, Rania got up and felt slightly better. She told Mohammed that she wanted to go back to her apartment in Barnes and prepare to travel back to Cairo.

'Are you sure you're ready Rania' he asked.

'No, but I've got to make an effort. You've both been very kind to me and you have to get back to Cairo for treatment.'

'The doctors say that there should be no problem in delaying my next chemotherapy session, so don't worry about us my dear' said Magda.

'But I do worry. In fact I worry about everything Magda. I think you should go as soon as possible. That will be a weight off my mind. But I need to go to Barnes and sort my life out. I need to go now while I'm feeling slightly better.'

'Okay said Mohammed, but I'm coming with you. You still need protection and the police don't seem to be doing much.'

'That's very kind of you Mohammed, but I think I can manage.'

'Nonsense' said Magda 'let Mohammed go with you.'

After some argument Rania agreed to Mohammed accompanying her but insisted that once she'd settled in, he would return to Magda.

'I'm not leaving you alone. I want to be assured that you'll have support in your apartment. I'm sure your two friends will be able to help?'

'We'll see' said Rania. 'Now, let's make a move.'

Mohammed packed a small suitcase and phoned for a cab. Rania packed what little she had, kissed Magda goodbye and waited at the front door. Within minutes the cab rolled up to the apartment block and the two of them took their seats in the back. The cab drove off.

Thomas DeVelt, who was hiding behind a tree opposite the apartment block, put his helmet on and followed them on his motorbike.

CHAPTER THIRTY-ONE

Joshua Wilson-Smith, Head of MI5, was summoned to the PM's office at Number 10. He was chauffeur driven to Downing Street whereupon, on reaching his destination, got out of his Jaguar and told his driver to park in the local NCP car park. He would call him when he was ready.

He went up to the main gates and spoke to the policeman on duty. He showed him his identity card and, after completing the visitor's book, strolled up to Number 10. Another policeman checked his credentials and allowed him to walk through to the hallway. Joshua had visited Number 10 on many occasions and took little notice of the grand decor as he walked up the stairs to the PM's private office. He knocked on the door and waited.

'Come in' a voice commanded.

Joshua walked in and faced a sea of sombre faces. Sitting behind a highly polished antique table was the PM accompanied at his side by the Home Secretary and Chief Constable of the Metropolitan Police.

'Sit down Joshua' said the PM. 'We don't need any introductions do we. We all know each other after all?'

'Yes sir' said Joshua.

'Good, then let's get to the point of this meeting. But before we do, anyone for tea?'

'No thanks' they all said in unison.

'Right, Joshua, we have a problem. Have you any idea what that problem might be?'

'No sir.'

'Well, the problem is you.' There was a pause 'Do you know why Joshua?'

'Haven't a clue sir.'

'Well let me explain. You see there's a fine line between getting the job done and getting the job done without fuss and publicity. You may be *getting the job done* but, unfortunately, you're causing too much *fuss and publicity*. Do you know where I'm going on this one Joshua?'

'No sir.'

'Then that's a pity because if you don't know, then we have even a bigger problem than I first thought. Do you want me to spell it out?'

'Yes sir.'

'Okay, let's start from the beginning. You were tasked with sorting out the Rania Hakim and Inspector Othman problem were you not?'

'Yes sir'

'What did you think that meant?'

'I agreed with the Home Secretary that they would be silenced.'

'What, you mean killed?'

'Yes sir.'

'And did you agree to this Home Secretary?'

'Of course not sir. I wanted them out of the way but I never mentioned anything about killing them. That was Joshua's interpretation.'

'You knew what I had in mind Home Secretary. Had the killings went smoothly with the minimum of fuss we wouldn't be sitting here today.'

'That's not the point 'said the Home Secretary. 'I suggested that they be repatriated to Cairo or dealt with in some other way but I didn't sanction their killing.'

'You let me get on with it. As I said, had there not been various cock ups, I wouldn't be sitting here. At the end of the day, I did my job in support of the government in the most effective way.'

'It was hardly effective Joshua' said the PM. 'At the end of the day your operative killed three innocent people and has yet to complete his mission. I assume that Rania Hakim is still in this country?'

'We think so sir, yes' said the Home Secretary.

'Right, so your operative killed the Professor, killed Inspector Othman, and, through his bungling, allowed the press to publicise the whole sordid affair?'

'Yes sir' said Joshua.

'What about this Samantha Wilson character, has she got anything to do with your operative Joshua – and you'd better tell me the truth, it could save a lot of time.'

'Yes sir. I believe operative Thomas DeVelt raped, assaulted and then murdered Ms Wilson. He phoned to tell me. Evidently she had taped all their conversations and when Thomas found out, he went berserk.'

'When he told you all this, did you tell the police?'

'The police knew he was suspected of assaulting and raping Sam, but I told them to hold off until he'd completed his mission. That was the first occasion. When he told me he'd murdered her I spoke to the Chief Constable but didn't mention Thomas's name. When the murder was revealed in the papers, I knew I had to come clean and told the Home Secretary everything.'

'So Thomas DeVelt murdered Samantha Wilson?'

'Yes Peter.'

'And you withheld this evidence from me, presumably because you wanted DeVelt to complete his mission.'

'That's about the size of it.'

'The world's gone mad' said Peter. 'Basically Joshua, you've lost all sense of proportion. When the government instructs MI5 on a matter of national security it doesn't give you the right as Head to sanction murder. You've got a maniac operative on the loose who's probably contemplating the murder of Rania Hakim.'

'I don't think so. I fired him and told him to disappear.'

'So what? This murderer is on the loose. He's got nothing to lose and, by what you've told us, is completely out of control.'

'I know sir, but don't forget the bigger picture – despite Thomas's madness – Rania Hakim killed the Head of MI5.'

'I know that Josh, in fact we all know that, but for political reasons, we're letting that one go. Put that to one side will you?'

'Okay sir. All I can say, and I address this to you Peter, is that this is now a police matter. I'll keep out of it. I suggest you try to find young Thomas straight away.'

'Fine, but where is he?'

'Rania Hakim lives in Barnes. I suggest you get your men down there now.'

Peter Falkner made for the door and was just about to exit when he stopped and turned around:

'And what about you Joshua? You sanctioned these killings, delayed investigations and withheld evidence from the police. In my book you're no better than this psychotic killer, Develt. You're no more than a criminal in my book and as such should be dealt with under my jurisdiction.'

'Okay Peter calm down' said the PM. 'We understand what you're saying, but we must handle this matter with a degree of sensitivity. Joshua's first objective was and is to preserve national security. As far as I can see he has intended to do this. He had the best of intentions for his country. Unfortunately his judgement in picking DeVelt was fraught to say the least. Leave this matter with me Peter and go and catch the bad guys.'

Peter looked at the PM and then the Home Secretary. He shook his head and said:

'You're wrong, all of you. You've lost sight of what matters. Your objective, whatever that was, could have been achieved without murdering three innocent people. You're all as guilty as each other. You say that I should catch the bad guys. Let me ask you this question: who are the bad guys?'

'I'll put that down as an overreaction Peter' said the PM. ' The government didn't sanction these killings and nor do we condone them. Your accusations are uncalled for. You're obviously emotional, and I understand that. But we are where we are and I suggest you calm down and get on with your job.'

'I'm sorry sir and I retract those comments. But I find it very frustrating when the Head of MI5 plays God and withholds information from the police – especially when it's a police matter.'

'I understand that Peter and your point is duly noted.'

Peter left the room and phoned Inspector Nigel Francis. Unfortunately, he got the engaged signal and had to leave a message - he told him to get down to Barnes as fast he could and arrest DeVelt for murder and rape. They could worry about the details later.

Nigel responded to the message about 20 minutes later.

'Where have you been? I put a call out for you about 20 minutes ago. DeVelt is your man. He raped, assaulted and then murdered Samantha Wilson and, if it's not already too late, he plans to murder Rania Hakim. Bring him in.'

'Sorry sir - involved in a bit of a crisis down at the station and couldn't respond. I'll get a couple of squad cars down there straightaway.'

'Good, make sure your officers are armed.'

Meanwhile, back in the PM's office, Joshua was asked to wait outside while the two of them deliberated on what to do. After about half an hour they called him back into the room.

'You've shown extraordinary bad judgement Josh although we believe your heart is in the right place. That's why we're not going to sack you. Treat this as a final warning but carry on the good work. I suggest from now you check with the Home Secretary regarding your instructions before making any final decisions and, I suggest, you involve the Chief Constable a little bit more. We should all be singing from the same hymn sheet you know. You should take a holiday, lie low for three or four weeks, you've earned it.'

'Thank you sir. What about the criminal charges Peter alluded to?'

'Oh, don't worry about that, I'll have a word with him. I'm sure we can make an exception in your case, after all, you are the Head of MI5.'

'And what about Rania Hakim sir. When all is said and done, she did kill Sir Michael. We can't let her get away with this can we?'

'Of course not old boy. Let's hope Thomas gets to her before our trusted police force, or should I say service Home Secretary?'

'You should sir.'

'Right that will be all Josh. And remember, next time select an operative who is a little more discreet. We don't like things of this nature ending up in the press. In fact, perhaps Thomas needs to go on some courses which teach him the art of handling things discreetly or, more to the point, doing things without anybody knowing. We don't call it the Secret Service for nothing do we? We like his enthusiasm but loathe his indiscretions. Sort it out Josh will you old chap?'

'But I've sacked him sir.'

'Well re-engage him, give him some training and set him off again on some other project.'

'Certainly sir.'

CHAPTER THIRTY-TWO

Rania and Mohammed arrived in Barnes around 4.00 pm. It was a sunny afternoon and the high street was busy; mothers or fathers with their children stopping for coffee on their way home having picked up their kids from school; people of all ages scurrying round the shops, buying snacks or drinks, having completed their part time jobs; lorry drivers delivering their last loads of the day and frustrating oncoming motorists as they waited patiently for the lorries to move on – the high street buzzed with excitement although Rania was oblivious to everything apart from looking forward to opening her front door and chilling out on her sofa.

They passed the pond and noticed a swan followed by an entourage of cygnets making their way across the pavement, obviously confused by the direction their mother was taking them. On lookers gave them a wide berth as they waddled down the road until they reached a curb, at which point the mother realised her predicament and led her babies back to the edge of the pond. They then entered the water and nonchalantly paddled towards the centre without, it seemed, a care in the world. Rania gazed enviously at them and wished her life was as simple. *Do we make life complicated or does life make our lives complicated,* she thought. Which came first? She concluded that it was a combination of both and decided to concentrate on her immediate predicament – was she to stay or go or to end it all? Her head was pounding with thoughts she couldn't control which added to her anxieties which returned her to her thoughts which she couldn't control and which added to her anxieties – a vicious circle which she couldn't break. She was feeling bad again.

At last they arrived at her apartment block and both Mohammed and Rania offered to pay the fare. After some discussion between the two of them, the driver was eventually paid and drove off leaving them standing in the street with suitcases in hand. Rania unlocked the front door and invited Mohammed into her apartment.

'Well Mohammed, this is my lounge and there is the kitchen. The loo is down the hallway.'

'Very nice Rania but where do your friends live?'

'They live upstairs but I doubt whether they're about at this time.'

'Well, I'm not leaving you until I know you're safe.'

'I'm fine Mohammed. Do you want a cup of tea?'

⇥⇤

Meanwhile Thomas DeVelt waited patiently at the corner of the road. He'd seen the two of them enter Rania's apartment and decided to wait to see whether the man was going to stay or go. He had no intention of killing both of them but, if the man were to stay, he might have to commit a double murder. He had secured his money from James Nathan and, once this mission had been completed, he could be satisfied that he'd done his duty for *Queen and Country,* could make his exit and be gone forever.

Previously he had found a door at the back of the apartment block which, with a bit of force, he'd unlocked. It was clear that this door hadn't been used for ages and the locks had got so rusty that the metal was disintegrating. Once through the door he'd found himself in a small back garden which hadn't been maintained for years. The grass was overgrown and what used to be flower beds were now homes for weeds and, indeed, dumping grounds for domestic rubbish. He'd made his way through this jungle until he'd reached a window which, on looking in, he'd reckoned was Rania's bedroom. He could easily and silently punch a hole in the glass and unlock the window allowing him to make access into her flat.

What he must do now is wait.

⊨⊨ ⊨⊨

Rania had made at least three cups of tea for Mohammed before insisting that he should go back to Magda.

'But will you be all right Rania?' he asked.

'Of course Mohammed. I just need to be alone for a couple of days to figure out what I'm going to do. You go back to Cairo, I insist, and get Magda to complete her treatment. You've got my number so phone me when you arrive.'

They hugged each other and Mohammed left. Thomas observed him as he made his way to Barnes station. He checked his pistol and made his way to the back of Rania's apartment.

Rania unpacked her suitcase and set her medication on her dressing table. She sat down and looked at herself in the mirror. She had changed. There was grey hair forming at the crown of her head and specks of white were apparent on the edges of her long black hair which framed a rather haggard face. She looked very tired with black circles forming under her eyes. She'd lost weight which added to her general gauntness. Her hands trembled as she opened a drawer and took out a bottle of vodka. She placed this on the dressing table. She found a glass in another drawer and poured a generous measure. She swallowed this in one gulp and winced as she felt the effect. Tears ran down her cheek as she thought of Rob, Angus and Othman – all good men who had died supporting her. She had killed and whether this was right or wrong, what right did she have in taking another's life? She did it out of revenge in righting a terrible wrong exacted on the only man she'd loved. Was this sufficient justification? Would Allah see it that way? There were too many bad thoughts running through her mind. She couldn't control them. They would haunt her forever. She tried to think about her childhood growing up in the suburbs of Baghdad – good times which were lost forever. She thought about her loving parents and felt guilty about her failure to keep in contact – she would miss them dearly. She felt the blackness returning. She couldn't control her feelings – she felt herself going down and down – down to a place which caused unbearable agitation and helplessness. She didn't want to go back there – it would be too painful. She had to stop it – she had to do the right thing. She took another gulp of vodka and swallowed all thirty tablets. After a few minutes she became dizzy. Her stomach ached. She took the bottle and swallowed what was left. She sat and gazed at herself in the mirror. Time stood still. Eventually she stood up and made her way towards her bed. She couldn't walk properly; everything was in slow motion; everything was blurred. The bed was far away. No matter how hard she tried, she couldn't get to it. She grabbed the duvet and collapsed on the floor. She felt nothing, she saw nothing – only blackness.

Nigel Francis had ordered two police cars with armed officers to get down to Barnes without delay. They had already lost about 30 minutes owing to the confusion at the station. This was caused by Lyn, his number two, who had swung her buttocks once too many times, and was now claiming sexual harassment. One of the young bucks decided to smack her bum as she walked out of the canteen and this had created havoc at the station. Unfortunately Nigel had got himself involved and this had distracted him, albeit momentarily – or so he thought, while he calmed things down. He'd already formed a view that it was probably six of one and half a dozen of the other, which was a shame, because when he confronted Lyn with this diagnosis, she went berserk!

'I'm the victim here sir and you should know better.'

'Okay Lyn, write out a report and we'll get it sorted. But you do tend to provoke these guys don't you?'

That was it. Lyn threw a tantrum and vanished into the ladies. Nigel decided to let things calm down and listened to his messages. That's when he'd picked up the message from the Chief Constable. *Shit* he thought and made for his BMW – he could activate resources while driving down to Barnes. He had the address recorded in his note book but he needed to contact Rania straightaway. He phoned her but got no answer. *Shit* he said again as he passed red traffic lights and switched on his siren.

Thomas entered the back garden and peered through Rania's window. He couldn't see anything apart from her bed. The duvet looked as though it had been tossed aside. He quickly scored a circle in the glass with his diamond pointed punch and removed a segment of glass making little noise in the process. He then reached in with his right hand and unlocked the window. He got himself through the gap with surprisingly little difficulty, bearing in mind the size of his frame. Thanks to many years of rugby and regular gym workouts, he was still in good condition and could match anyone for strength and stamina. When he entered the room he saw a leg sticking out from under the bed. He took out his pistol and moved quickly towards Rania's body. She lay there unconscious. He looked around and saw an empty bottle on the dressing table. He went over to the table and noticed an empty box of tablets. He didn't recognise the name of the medication but guessed it was for depression. *What luck* he thought. She'd killed herself. Saved him a job. He went over to her and felt for a pulse. It was very feeble but she was alive. He listened to her faint breathing. He remembered finding Katerine in the Rob Williams affair and felt blessed that he could simply leave Rania to die as he had done with the fatally wounded Katerine. But Rania might recover. He could take no chances. A quick bullet to the head should do it. He drew out his pistol and fitted the silencer. He pointed the gun towards her temple and was about to fire when a loud shattering noise distracted him ... in an instant three armed policemen rushed through the door shouting 'Stop. Put that weapon down.' Thomas did so:

'You've got it wrong guys' he shouted. 'I'm MI5 and this lady murdered Sir Michael Wilkinson.'

'Yeah', said the tallest policeman 'and my name's *Mickey Mouse*. Now drop your weapon and put both hands on your head...do it now.'

'Okay, okay but phone Joshua Wilson–Smith. He sanctioned this. I'm just doing my job.'

'And what about Samantha Wilson Mr DeVelt? Were you just doing your job when you raped and murdered her?' asked Nigel as he casually entered the room.

'You've no proof. I deny it. I'm an MI5 operative and you can't touch me.'

'I arrest you for the rape and murder of Samantha Wilson, the murders of Professor Lear and Inspector Othman and the attempted murder of Rania Hakim. You ...'

'Forget the arresting crap. I'm protected. You're making a big mistake.'

'Handcuff him Joe and get him down to the station. I'll see to things here.'

Nigel went over to Rania who was regaining consciousness. She looked very pale and held a pained expression on her face. Her eyes opened and closed in quick succession as if she were unsure as to what had happened and unsure as to where she was.

'You've got to get up Rania. We've got to get you walking around.'

She managed to get up with Nigel's help and tried to steady herself. She stared at him with a wild look on her face. She then collapsed in his arms, the contents of her stomach spilling over his best shoes.

'Thank God you're alive' he said 'No one's vomited over me before – I'll take that as a gesture of fondness – we're obviously destined to be partners. Bill, get the ambulance down here.'

Nigel helped her on to her bed. She lay there very still. She was pale and gaunt. In fact she looked like she had died. But she hadn't died and her attempted suicide, if that's what it was, had failed. She closed her eyes and then opened them. Her senses had returned. She didn't see or feel blackness anymore. She noticed the light pouring in from her window. For the first time in several weeks she felt a sense of hopefulness, a sense of optimism- although she didn't know why. Perhaps she'd just had a near death experience and it had made her realise that life might be worth living after all. Nevertheless, her head began to pound and she prepared herself for the king of all hangovers.

EPILOGUE

Thomas and indeed his solicitor made several attempts to phone Joshua Wilson-Smith without success. Messages were left which stated that as the government and MI5 had sanctioned the killings of Inspector Othman and Rania Hakim, Thomas was simply carrying out his job and was immune from any criminal or civil prosecution. They also stated that the appropriate protection should be given with regard to the rape and murder of Samantha Wilson as she was threatening to disclose details of his confidential work as an MI5 operative, and that any such breach would have been tantamount to treason. Lastly, they pointed out that if he were convicted and summoned to trial, he, through his legal representatives, would be requesting the PM, Home Secretary and Head of MI5 to attend to give evidence and be cross examined in public.

Needless to say Thomas was intent on *blowing the whistle* and would take any action necessary to bring the authorities down unless all charges were withdrawn. Individual letters were sent to the Chief Constable as well as those mentioned above which set out the case. Essentially, this stated that as Thomas was a government agent working for the government under orders from MI5, he was, in fact, immune from any judicial proceedings.

There then ensued a row between all parties on the question of whether an MI5 operative could be charged under UK criminal law for acts sanctioned by the employer (in this case the government and/or MI5) in pursuit of national security.

The government's response was quite straightforward: it didn't sanction any rape, any killing or, indeed any 'criminal activity'. Indeed it was unaware that any such acts were taking place. Had it become aware, it would have regarded such acts as falling under UK criminal law and any claim for individual immunity would have been crushed. The government was quite certain that the alleged acts committed by Thomas, including the murders of Professor Lear and Samantha Wilson, could not be protected in any way and that the rule of law had to apply. It went on to state that, if called upon by the courts, the relevant ministers, including the PM, would attend proceedings to give such evidence.

The Head of MI5 gave a similar response which, together with the government's, gave Thomas's legal representatives a challenging brief, to put it mildly! Any money Thomas had accumulated, through foul means or legitimate earnings, would have been spent on lawyer fees.

The authorities needn't have worried. On 15th October 2004 Thomas Develt was found dead having hanged himself in his apartment.

On the other hand James Nathan did go to court and was found guilty of fraud and medical malpractice. He was given a two year prison sentence and struck off the medical register. He was also ordered to pay damages to Magda Ishmail amounting to £150,000. His counterpart in Cairo, Mr Maximilian Gustav was also found guilty and was given similar punishments in Cairo.

As for Rania, Nigel, the Ishmails and their teenage children, they all attended Othman's funeral in the desert suburbs of Khartoum. There were many members of his family in attendance, not to mention a great many friends. He was buried by the side of his father, although unlike his father's, his coffin was closed during the ceremonies. The gravestone had already been erected and stood proudly, if that's the right word, by his father's.

When the entourage had completely disappeared Othman came out from the shadows of the trees. He'd witnessed his own funeral which gave him a very weird sensation. He went up to his grave and rubbed his back which was giving him gip. The stitches in his neck needed removing and soon he would have to re enter the world of the living. Nigel had advised him to stay low for a couple of months and then to contact him. By that time he would have disclosed the whole story to the chief – a man he could trust – and, hopefully, Othman's services could be put to good use – if, of course, he were interested.

Othman looked at his gravestone and pondered on the date of his death – 15th September 2004. It gave him a sense of doom, gloom and finality even though he was still alive. He decided to score out the date with his knife - it didn't feel right; but just as he was about to make the first cut he was distracted by teenage voices:

'Hello Uncle Othman. We thought you were dead but obviously you're not'. Othman nearly jumped out of his skin. He was speechless. They looked at each other and smiled. There was a further pause as they all stared at his gravestone. Chinaz broke the silence: ' Now tell us one of your fantastic stories and explain to us how one minute you're dead and the next minute you're alive – and don't exaggerate like you normally do.'

Othman told them his story and got them to swear that they wouldn't tell anyone. He explained that he had unfinished detective work to do and it was essential his cover wasn't blown. They agreed and went back to join the funeral party. He knew he could trust them to keep quiet. In telling the story he concluded that it was probably best to let the world think he was dead – at least for the time being. He could use this to his own advantage in hunting down the bad guys; or, in any event, that's what he figured. He left the graveyard leaving the date of death intact for all to see. He then disappeared into the desert wasteland, walking in the opposite direction of the funeral party.

After a few minutes Rania returned to the grave to spend a few minutes alone with Othman. Even though he was dead she sensed that one day she would meet him, along with Angus and Rob in a different world. She listened to the silence of the desert. There was no one around. The funny thing was that as she listened she was sure she heard a clucking noise coming from the ground. It was very distinct and definitely sounded like a chicken. How strange, she thought and walked away.

www.ingramcontent.com/pod-product-compliance
Lightning Source LLC
Chambersburg PA
CBHW051414170626
46809CB00006B/2156